Hi, I'm JIMMY!

Like me, you probably noticed the world is run by adults.
But ask yourself: Who would do the best job
of making books that *kids* will love?
Yeah. **Kids!**

So that's how the idea of JIMMY books came to life.
We want every JIMMY book to be so good
that when you're finished, you'll say,
"PLEASE GIVE ME ANOTHER BOOK!"

Give this one a try and see if you agree.
(If not, you're probably an adult!)

JIMMY PATTERSON BOOKS
FOR YOUNG READERS

James Patterson Presents

Sci-Fi Junior High by John Martin and Scott Seegert

Sci-Fi Junior High: Crash Landing by John Martin and Scott Seegert

How to Be a Supervillain by Michael Fry

How to Be a Supervillain: Born to Be Good by Michael Fry

The Unflushables by Ron Bates

Ernestine, Catastrophe Queen by Merrill Wyatt

The Middle School Series by James Patterson

Middle School, The Worst Years of My Life

Middle School: Get Me Out of Here!

Middle School: Big Fat Liar

Middle School: How I Survived Bullies, Broccoli, and Snake Hill

Middle School: Ultimate Showdown

Middle School: Save Rafe!

Middle School: Just My Rotten Luck

Middle School: Dog's Best Friend

Middle School: Escape to Australia

Middle School: From Hero to Zero

The I Funny Series by James Patterson

I Funny

I Even Funnier

I Totally Funniest

I Funny TV

I Funny: School of Laughs

I Funny: Around the World

The Treasure Hunters Series by James Patterson

Treasure Hunters

Treasure Hunters: Danger Down the Nile

For exclusives, trailers, and other information,
visit jimmypatterson.org

NOT SO NORMAL NORBERT

JAMES PATTERSON
with Joey Green
Illustrated by Hatem Aly

JIMMY Patterson Books
LITTLE, BROWN AND COMPANY
New York Boston London

Text copyright © 2018 by James Patterson
Illustrations copyright © 2018 by Hatem Aly

JIMMY Patterson Books / Little, Brown and Company
Hachette Book Group
1290 Avenue of the Americas, New York, NY 10104
jimmypatterson.org

First Edition: July 2018

JIMMY Patterson Books is an imprint of Little, Brown and Company, a division of Hachette Book Group, Inc. The Little, Brown name and logo are trademarks of Hachette Book Group, Inc. The JIMMY Patterson Books® name and logo are trademarks of JBP Business, LLC.

The Hachette Speakers Bureau provides a wide range of authors for speaking events. To find out more, go to hachettespeakersbureau.com or call (866) 376-6591.

Library of Congress Cataloging-in-Publication Data

Names: Patterson, James, author. | Green, Joey, author.
Title: Not so normal Norbert / James Patterson and Joey Green; illustrated by Hatem Aly.
Description: First edition. | New York : Little, Brown and Company, 2018. | "JIMMY Patterson Books." | Summary: Having been judged Different, Norbert, Drew, and Sophie are banished from the United State of Earth to Astro-Nuts Camp on Zorquat 3 in the Orion Nebula, interfering with Norbert's quest to find his parents.
Identifiers: LCCN 2017026846| ISBN 978-0-316-46541-0 (hardcover) |
Subjects: | CYAC: Behavior—Fiction. | Conformity—Fiction. | Friendship—Fiction. | Missing persons—Fiction. | Life on other planets—Fiction. | Science fiction. | Humorous stories.
Classification: LCC PZ7.P27653 Not 2018 | DDC [Fic]—dc23

10 9 8 7 6 5 4 3 2 1

LSC-C

Printed in the United States of America

For Ashley and Julia
—JG

NOT SO NORMAL NORBERT

Prologue

"I pledge subservience to Loving Leader of the United State of Earth, and to the ground on which he stands, one planet under surveillance, invincible, with conformity and security for all."

We're all standing at attention, holding up two fingers to make the letter V, and saying a bunch of meaningless words to the TruthScreen at the front of our classroom.

We do this every morning. It's ridiculous, if you ask me, but I keep my mouth shut. Well, not when I'm saying the pledge.

You can't complain about saying the pledge. If you do, the Truth Police burst in and arrest you, and that's not something you really want. Unless you're crazy, which I'm definitely not.

I'm in seventh grade at Middle School Number 1022 in Region 154. Our school is painted gray. The sky is gray. The clouds are gray. My classmates and I all wear the same exact gray jumpsuits and the same gray expressions on our faces. I guess you could say we're color coordinated.

Our gray jumpsuits aren't school uniforms or anything. Everyone on Earth wears them to make us all equal. Even His All-Knowing Eternal Excellency, Loving Leader, wears a gray jumpsuit.

He's on the TruthScreen right now. He's very serious. His white hair is pretty wild. His eyes are really intense. Fierce. Penetrating. He's not exactly the kind of guy you'd want to run into in a dark alley.

After saying the pledge, we all sit down at our school desks in unison. Just like we do every morning. It's time to listen to Loving Leader's daily Declaration of Dependence.

Thrilling.

"My fellow earthlings," says Loving Leader. "Conformity makes us free. Free to conform. Because we all know different is dangerous. Different is diabolical. Different is a disease. Yes, a disease detrimental to our way of life. A disease that destroys the equality we've fought so hard to win. And what causes this horrible disease? The evils of individuality. The wicked spark of imagination. The foul stench of creativity. Shoot for the moon, my friends, and what happens? You explode in a deadly fireball and get burned to a crisp. Individuality is an illness. Imagination is insanity. Creativity is crazy. Originality threatens our way of life...."

He goes on and on and on. Blah, blah, blahbity blah. Naturally, my mind wanders, and I look out the window at those gray clouds in the gray sky and start thinking back to when I was a little kid. I remember my father playing catch with me, and my mother singing a lullaby before tucking me into bed and kissing me good night.

"You there!" shouts Loving Leader. "You, staring out the window!"

I nearly jump out of my skin. I turn my head from the window and look at the TruthScreen, giving Loving Leader my undivided attention.

"You're not daydreaming, are you?" asks Loving Leader, pointing his finger directly at yours truly.

"M-me?" I stammer.

"Yes, you! Norbert Riddle, Person Number L4LUZR-1."

"No, Your All-Knowing Eternal Excellency. I would *never* dream of daydreaming."

"Good," he says. "Because daydreaming is one of

the three deadly warning signs of imagination. And we all know that imagination is...what?"

"Insanity!" shouts everyone in my class. Including me.

Loving Leader smiles widely. In a creepy sort of way. "To remain free, we must all conform, we must stamp out our uniqueness for the greater good," he says. "Remember, Loving Leader sees all, knows all, and loves all." He holds up two fingers to make the letter *V*. The TruthScreen goes black.

Our teacher, mean old Mrs. Hurlbutt, tells us that she's visiting the lavatory, which is a fancy way of saying she needs to use the bathroom. "I expect you all to be on your best behavior while I'm gone, so no one gets arrested by the Truth Police and mysteriously disappears, never to be heard from again. Like Norbert's parents!"

All my classmates gasp.

I can't believe Mrs. Hurlbutt just said that. She's a horrible teacher. And a horrible person. Yeah, the Truth Police took away my parents when I was a little kid. But that's none of her business. I'm the one who lost my mother and father. I'm the one forced to grow up without the two most important people in my life. I'm the one stuck living with my boring aunt and uncle.

Now I'm steaming mad. At Mrs. Hurlbutt. At Loving Leader. At this stupid school. At everything!

Enough is enough! I'll show them!

The minute that nasty old biddy steps into the hallway, I rise to my feet, walk to the front of the classroom, and stand on top of Mrs. Hurlbutt's desk. Everyone in the class stares at me. Then I mess up my mop of dark hair to look like Loving Leader.

"My fellow earthlings," I say, doing my best impression. "Conformity is the freedom to wear gray jumpsuits like everyone else. The freedom to think like everyone else. The freedom to agree with everything I say. The freedom to be sheep. *Baaa! Baaa! Baaa!*"

Everyone stares at me in complete shock. They can't believe I'm actually making fun of Loving Leader. No one says anything. They're too scared to even crack a smile.

Until a kid named Drew Weaver bursts out laughing.

Then everyone else starts chuckling too, nervously

at first, then hysterically, giving me the green light to keep going. Suddenly I'm on a roll.

"As Your All-Knowing Eternal Excellency, I say this: My planet, my rules. The world belongs to me. The earth, the moon, the planets, the stars. They're mine. All mine. Fear me, obey me, love me, and together we'll make the world safe for mediocrity. Like I always say, creativity stinks! Imagination stinks! Originality stinks! Remember, Loving Leader smelt it, because Loving Leader dealt it." I hold up two fingers to make the letter *L*—for "loser."

Laughter fills the room. Drew applauds, and the other kids join in, smiling widely. I feel like I'm on top of the world. Even though I'm only on top of Mrs. Hurlbutt's desk.

Suddenly flashing red lights drop from the ceiling and start whirling.

Everyone goes completely silent. They immediately sit up at attention, fold their hands on their desks, and stare straight ahead.

"What's going on?" I ask. "Is this some sort of fire drill?"

I look to Drew. He shrugs. He doesn't know either.

Sirens start screaming. The Truth Police burst through the door, pointing these big laser guns at me. They surround me. Without warning, Loving Leader appears on the TruthScreen and points his finger at me. "Loving Leader sees all, knows all, and loves all."

"You're under arrest," say the Truth Police, "for being different." They slap handcuffs on my wrists and drag me from the room.

Was it something I said?

part one

Chapter 1

The Truth Police take me to a gray building, where they hold me tight by both arms and usher me down a long, arched corridor filled with cobwebs. The dirty stone walls are lined on both sides with thick steel prison doors. A rat scurries along a pipe hanging from the ceiling.

The thought of being thrown in the slammer and left to rot really gives me the creeps. But I'm not nervous. I'm too terrified to be nervous.

Finally the Truth Police stop. One officer punches a bunch of numbers into a keypad. The door to a cell pops open. They throw me inside without taking off my handcuffs and slam the door shut. *Bam!* Something tells me this can't be good.

My prison cell? Cold, tiny, and gloomy. It almost reminds me of home.

Home is 526 Dreary Lane in a dreary little house with my dreary aunt Martha and my dreary uncle Hank.

They're really not that bad. I'm just kidding around. I love Aunt Martha and Uncle Hank like crazy. Which just goes to show, maybe I really am crazy.

But they're definitely two of the dullest people I've ever met. And believe me, I've met a lot of dull people. Mostly at Middle School Number 1022.

Aunt Martha works as an inventory clerk at a thumbtack warehouse. Incredibly boring, if you ask me. But Aunt Martha can't stop talking about the day they had a big spill in aisle 70.

Uncle Hank has a job watching a machine on an assembly line insert cotton into aspirin bottles. He sits there, making sure the proper amount of cotton goes into each bottle. He loves the excitement.

At home Aunt Martha and Uncle Hank spend all their time watching shows on the TruthScreen. There's only one channel, which makes it a lot easier to watch the same shows everyone else watches. Also, having just one channel means we never fight over which show we're going to watch. So I suppose that helps create family harmony.

The TruthScreen, as you may have guessed, is a two-way screen. We watch it. And it watches us. So Loving Leader can keep us safe—from ourselves. Like he says, "You're your own worst enemy." And based on the fact that I'm now sitting in a cold, dank prison cell, I guess Loving Leader was definitely right about that.

You're probably wondering why I live with my aunt and uncle. Especially since they're so boring and dull.

What happened to my parents?

That's a long story. I really don't want to get into the details, but I was five years old when my parents disappeared. I've been trying to find them for the last seven years—with no luck whatsoever.

Aunt Martha and Uncle Hank are no help, either.

They're too scared of Loving Leader to even talk about my parents. They don't want to end up in a prison cell. Like this one.

"The walls have ears," Aunt Martha likes to say.

Then Uncle Hank points at the TruthScreen. "Eyes, too," he says.

I desperately want to track down my mother and father. I miss them something awful. I'm determined to find them. Of course, there's no way I can look for them if I'm stuck inside a prison cell. I guess I should have thought of that before I climbed up on Mrs. Hurlbutt's desk.

I never expected to get arrested for doing my impression of Loving Leader. When Mrs. Hurlbutt left the classroom, I figured the coast was clear. Too bad I forgot about the TruthScreen. I mean, sure, Loving Leader constantly says he "sees all, knows all, and loves all," but I didn't really think he'd have his eyes on our class. Besides, if Loving Leader really does love *all,* you'd think that would include a good laugh once in a while. Obviously, the guy can't take a joke. Stupid me.

I spend the next few hours sitting on the cold

floor of my cell, worrying about what's going to happen to me. Will I disappear like my parents did, never to be heard from again? How do I get out of here?

I wonder how long I'll be left all alone in this cell. Three hours? Three years? Forever? Or just until the end of time?

Now I fear for my life. I feel like I've been sitting in this cell for an eternity. Not that I know what an eternity feels like.

I wonder if they have room service in here.

Chapter 2

I hear footsteps outside the door to my cell. They clomp down the long hallway, getting louder and louder.

"Get your filthy hands off me!" yells someone. "Let go, you big bully!"

The door to my cell suddenly pops open. My heart jumps—and does a double backflip.

The Truth Police toss someone else inside the cell with me. It's still dark in here, so I can barely see him. He falls to the floor. He's tall. Lanky. The door slams shut again. The footsteps clomp back down the long hallway.

It's that kid named Drew Weaver. The first one who laughed at my impression of Loving Leader. His wrists are handcuffed like mine, but that doesn't stop him from pounding his fists on the back of the door. "Let me out of here!" he yells. "I'm warning you! This is your last chance before I get *really* mad!"

I don't know Drew very well. In fact, I don't know him at all. Mrs. Hurlbutt once caught him doodling and sent him to the principal's office. But that's really all I know about him.

I'm definitely glad to see a fellow classmate. But Drew doesn't seem very happy to see me. In fact, he seems really cheesed off at me. I have no idea why.

"All I did was laugh at what you did," says Drew. "I wouldn't be here if you hadn't made me laugh! I'm not different! *You're* the one who's different!"

"I'm not different either," I say.

"Then why did you get up on that desk?"

"It's a long story." I don't feel like telling him. Not right now, anyway.

"I hate you, Norbert Riddle! You're the reason I'm in here. You should have never done what you did. Do you know what's going to happen to us now?"

"I haven't the slightest idea."

"I do," says Drew. "And it's not going to be pretty."

"How do *you* know?"

"I was sent to the principal's office last week, remember?"

"So?"

"The principal locked the door and strapped me into a big metal chair. Then she put this weird thing on my head."

"What kind of weird thing?"

"It was sort of like a helmet. Attached to all these strange wires and doodads. She pressed a button, and the helmet started whirring like mad. My eyes popped wide open. I couldn't shut my eyes, no matter how hard I tried."

Drew is making me really antsy. I feel my heart beating like crazy. "Did they erase your memory or something?" I ask.

Drew shakes his head no. "Worse," he says. "The principal pressed another button. A TruthScreen lowered from the ceiling and started showing tapes of Loving Leader making speech after speech after speech. I thought my head was going to explode. I must have been strapped in that chair for a solid week—with Loving Leader droning on forever. 'Imagination is insanity.' 'Creativity is crazy.' Until it was drilled into my head."

That doesn't sound great, but it really doesn't sound so horrible, either.

"But this is going to be worse," says Drew. "Much worse."

"What could be worse than this creepy old prison cell?" I ask.

"The Powder Room." Drew grins. He's freaking me out and the guy seems happy about it. What a weirdo.

I take the bait. "What's the Powder Room?"

"I thought you'd never ask." He smiles again. "It's a giant room three stories tall with white walls. A big thingamabob—like a giant mirrored disco ball—hangs from the ceiling. The guards push you to the middle of the room and make you stand on this raised platform lit from underneath, like the dance floor in some fancy nightclub. The device lowers from the ceiling and makes a high-pitched noise. The lights on the dance floor flicker. The thingamabob zaps you with a bright-pink laser beam, and—*kapowie!* There's nothing left of you but a small pile of bright-pink powder. That's why it's called…" Drew waits for me to finish his sentence.

"Okay, I get it." Now I'm shaking like a leaf on a tree. (Not that I've ever seen an actual tree in person. Or a leaf. I have seen pictures, though.) Drew has me totally on edge. Maybe that's what happened to my parents. Maybe the Truth Police took them to the Powder Room. The thought of my parents transformed into pink powder makes me want to cry.

"It's nothing to worry about," says Drew, trying to calm me down. "The laser beam just dehydrates your body into powder. The Truth Police vacuum up the pink powder, put it in a test tube, and place you in storage. They can bring you back to life anytime at all—by just adding water."

So now I have to find two test tubes of pink powder. Then I realize something horrible. If I'm turned into pink powder too, I'll never be able to find my parents.

Chapter 3

Suddenly the door to our cell bursts open. Two burly guards shackle my ankles together. They clutch my handcuffed arms and guide me down the dark stone hallway. My shackles clank and clatter.

I have no idea where they're taking me. My whole body is trembling in fear.

We turn down a gloomy corridor toward a green door. The first guard punches a bunch of numbers into a keypad. The thick door swings open. The rusty hinges squeak. My heart pounds.

The guards bring me into a courtroom with high

ceilings and mahogany walls. They usher me up some stairs to a raised platform, shove me inside a boxy cage, and lock me inside. How nice.

From inside the cage, I look around the courtroom. Aunt Martha and Uncle Hank are seated on one of the benches. Their faces look gray and nervous. They're wearing their drab gray jumpsuits. Of course, everyone in the courtroom is wearing drab gray jumpsuits. We are all total fashionistas—the bailiff, the twelve members of the jury. Even mean old Mrs. Hurlbutt. Yeah, she's here too. Lucky me.

My lawyer is not wearing a gray jumpsuit. That's because I don't have a lawyer. There's no lawyer to prosecute me either.

"All rise for the Honorable Judge Wright," says the bailiff. "Never wrong."

Everyone stands up. I'm already standing in this stupid cage.

Judge Wright enters the courtroom. He wears (surprise!) a drab gray jumpsuit and looks like a crusty old grouch. He makes mean old Mrs. Hurlbutt look like an absolute sweetheart. He sits behind his judicial bench—a tall desk that towers over the courtroom. He bangs his gavel to start my Truth Trial.

"Norbert Riddle, Person Number L4LUZR-1. You are charged with six counts of being different."

The TruthScreen on the wall behind the judge suddenly shows me performing my impression of Loving Leader. I have to admit I look pretty funny. I wonder if I can get a copy of that. I decide it's probably not a good idea to ask.

My teacher takes the witness stand. (She doesn't really take it anywhere. She steps inside it.)

The bailiff makes her raise her right hand and hold up two fingers to make the letter *V.* "Do you swear to twist the truth, the half-truth, and spout anything but the truth?" Okay, that's not really what the bailiff asks her, but you get the idea.

Mrs. Hurlbutt testifies against me for daydreaming in class. Not just that one time I told you about. But all the times. "He's always looking out the window into space. And we all know that's one of the three deadly warning signs of imagination."

My aunt and uncle try their best to defend me.

"He's really a good boy at home," says Aunt Martha.

"How long has the accused been daydreaming?" asks the judge.

"Not long," says Uncle Hank.

"So you admit Norbert Riddle daydreams."

"Your Honor, I didn't admit anything."

"So, then, you deny Norbert Riddle has been daydreaming."

"Yes," says Uncle Hank. "I mean, no. I don't deny anything."

"In other words, you admit he's been daydreaming."

"Uhhh . . ."

Done with Uncle Hank, the judge turns to my aunt. "And what about you, Martha Riddle? Do you deny your nephew has been daydreaming?"

"Yes," says Aunt Martha. "I deny it."

"Let the record show that Norbert Riddle daydreams, but his aunt Martha denies it."

"No, wait, that's not what I meant," says Aunt Martha.

"So you deny that you admit your nephew daydreams."

"Yes, that's correct…I think. I'm honestly not sure anymore."

"So you're not sure whether you know that Norbert Riddle daydreams."

Befuddled, Aunt Martha sits back down on the bench.

The judge turns to me. "Norbert Riddle, Person Number L4LUZR-1. Do you have anything to say for yourself?"

I grip the bars of my cage and try to stick my

head out, but my ears won't fit through the bars. I'm so tense I'm shaking. My handcuffs clang against the bars of the cage. The chains on my ankles rattle and clank.

"I'm not different," I say. "Really, I'm not anything special. I'm mediocre like everyone else. Honest. Please don't turn me into pink powder."

"Pink powder?" asks Judge Wright.

Aunt Martha and Uncle Hank look to each other, perplexed.

Mrs. Hurlbutt scrunches up her wrinkled face and makes a sour expression.

"Rest assured, I won't turn you into pink powder," says Judge Wright. He faces the jury. "How do you find the accused?"

In desperate need of a hug, I think. But I decide not to say that out loud.

I look to the twelve grown-ups in the jury box. All wearing dull gray jumpsuits and dour expressions on their faces. They turn their heads to look at one another. No one makes a peep. What will they decide? Am I toast?

Chapter 4

The captain of the jury stands up, straightens her gray jumpsuit, and looks to her fellow jurors. They bob their heads. They haven't muttered a word to one another the whole time, but now they're somehow signaling one another with silent nods.

The captain glares at me for a moment. It feels like her eyes are shooting poison darts at me. Then she turns to the judge. She quivers, afraid to utter a word.

Judge Wright sits up in his chair. "For the love of Loving Leader," he barks. "Spit it out."

The jury captain clears her throat. "We the jury find the accused...different and dangerous. Creative and crazy. Imaginative and insane."

The other members of the jury applaud and cheer. "Different! Dangerous!" they chant. "Different! Dangerous! Different! Dangerous!"

The judge bangs his gavel. "Order in the court," he demands. He hammers his gavel again. *Bam! Bam! Bam!*

My stomach churns. My head starts spinning. I think I'm going to be sick. I'm not different. I can't even imagine being imaginative. I'm just as gray and faceless as everyone else. Why won't anyone believe me? I'm not a lunatic. I'm not crazy. Really, I'm not. Special, maybe. But different? Hardly.

Judge Wright tells me to rise for sentencing. Can't he see I'm already standing? And *I'm* the crazy one? I don't think so.

I look to my aunt and uncle. They're in complete shock. Just like me. Tears run down Aunt Martha's face. Uncle Hank puts his arm around her. He reaches into the gray pocket of his gray jumpsuit and hands her his gray handkerchief. She wipes away her tears and blows her nose. Loudly, which makes me laugh. Aunt Martha does a great impression of a foghorn.

The judge bangs his gavel. "Norbert Riddle, Person Number L4LUZR-1. You are hereby banished *forever* from the planet. The United State of Earth hereby declares you a nonperson. You will be sent to the Astro-Nuts prison on planet Zorquat Three in the Orion Nebula—one thousand three hundred forty-seven light-years from here."

Me? Prison? On another planet? How will I ever find my parents if I'm sent to the other side of the galaxy?

"Aunt Martha! Uncle Hank!" I yell. "Help me! Please!"

My aunt and uncle stare at me in the cage. They look so sad. So dreary. So defeated. I tug at the metal bars, rattling my handcuffs, chains, and shackles. Aunt Martha and Uncle Hank say nothing. They're afraid to speak up in my defense. Scared to show even an inkling of emotion. Petrified that if they say what they're really thinking, they, too, risk being labeled different and dangerous.

They live in fear of Loving Leader and the Truth-Screen. Terrified of being arrested and taken away like my parents were. Never to be seen again.

Right then and there I get the feeling Aunt Martha and Uncle Hank know exactly what happened to my parents. I can see it in their eyes.

"Where are my parents?" I yell. "Tell me, please!"

Aunt Martha and Uncle Hank shake their heads with sadness.

"We have no idea where on Earth they are, Norbert," says Aunt Martha.

On *Earth?* If my parents are imprisoned somewhere on Earth, then I have to stay here, even if it means being turned into pink powder. I plead to Judge Wright. "Send me to the Powder Room! Please! Turn me into pink powder! Send me anywhere but another planet!"

"Norbert," says Uncle Hank. "You need to be sent away for your own good."

Aunt Martha nods. Reluctantly. She wipes her tears with Uncle Hank's gray handkerchief.

So my aunt and uncle agree with Judge Wright. They seem relieved that I've been sentenced to a nuthouse on another planet. I guess they figure my sentence could be worse. A lot worse.

The guards open the cage, remove my handcuffs and chains, and put me in a straitjacket. If you've never seen one, a straitjacket is like a pullover shirt with long sleeves that wrap around you to keep your arms tied to your body. It's used to confine a crazy person, but sometimes a magician will escape from one onstage.

The guards drag me away. Kicking and shouting.

Too bad I'm not a magician.

Chapter 5

'm back in my cold prison cell. Alone. Trapped in a straitjacket. And having a total panic attack. Although I have to admit, this straitjacket does keep me rather warm and cozy.

You're probably wondering where Drew went. When the guards threw me back in the cell, they grabbed Drew and dragged him, yelling and screaming, to his Truth Trial. I bet he's yelling and screaming at Judge Wright this very minute.

Meanwhile, I'm stuck all by my lonesome in this dungeon. The last place I want to be sent is across the universe to some desolate planet. There's only one thing for me to do. *Escape*. All I need is a decent plan. And a way out of this stupid straitjacket.

I wriggle and squirm. I twist and twirl.

The door pops open again. Two guards toss Drew back in the cell. They slam the door shut again.

Drew is wrapped in his own straitjacket. He's wiggling and squirming just like me.

"What happened to you?" I ask.

"The jury declared me different and dangerous."

"I don't understand. All you did was laugh at me. You didn't do anything creative or imaginative. I didn't either, really. But you *definitely* didn't."

"Well, that's not totally true. I doodle all the time. I can't stop. It's just something I do."

"Are they going to send you to the Powder Room?"

"No such luck," says Drew. "The judge banished me to a prison on Zorquat Three."

"Me too."

"Yeah, but there's just one problem."

"What's that?"

"There is no prison on Zorquat Three. They just want us to think we're being sent to a prison."

"How could you possibly know that?"

"Zorquat Three is a bleak planet covered with quicksand pits and giant, man-eating lizards. With forked tongues. And razor-sharp claws. They eat kids like you and me for breakfast. Everyone knows that." Now I'm sweating buckets.

Drew grins, like he's happy to see me with the heebie-jeebies. What's with this kid?

Suddenly the door to the cell bangs open....

Bright light from the stone corridor fills our prison cell. A big silhouette stands in the doorway. It steps forward, and I suddenly make out a large, gruff-looking man wearing a tight-fitting space suit and a Viking helmet. You know, one of those helmets with two sharp horns. Kind of kooky, if you ask me.

A patch on his uniform says his name is Grissom. He's got scraggly black hair and a trimmed black beard. Behind Grissom stand three robot guards aiming laser guns directly at us. The robots all look the same. They're thin, tall, and gold—with beady little red lights for eyes.

"So, you're the new Astro-Nuts," says Grissom. His voice sounds like gravel.

I turn to Drew. "What are Astro-Nuts?" I whisper.

Drew shrugs. "I guess *we* are," he says.

"Put a cork in it," snaps Grissom. "You two non-persons best not give me any trouble."

Grissom leads the way. We follow after him, still wearing our straitjackets. The three robot guards walk behind us, their laser guns aimed at our backs. I look for a way to escape, but I can feel the robots scrutinizing me with their piercing red eyes.

Grissom brings us outside to a sleek silver spaceship standing upright in the middle of a courtyard. The landing legs make the large spacecraft look like a spider.

"All aboard," shouts Grissom.

There's nowhere for us to go but up the ladder into the spaceship. Grissom follows us. The robots lower their laser guns and load huge metallic crates into the cargo hold.

Once we're aboard, Grissom removes our straitjackets and places Drew and me in the same clean white jail cell—with two cots, a sink, and a toilet. Across the hall is another barred cell containing one other nonperson.

"Boys, meet your fellow Astro-Nut," says Grissom. "Sophie Singer, this is Norbert Riddle and Drew Weaver."

Sophie Singer sits on the cot in her cell with her head buried in her hands. Her long, curly brown hair covers her face. She wears—you guessed it—a gray jumpsuit. Sophie just whimpers and refuses to look up at us.

Who is this strange girl? And what did she do to end up here?

Chapter 6

We zoom across the galaxy at some sort of mind-blowing super-duper-hyper-turbo-zippo-speed—a gazillion bajillion times the speed of light. Doggone fast. That's the technical term for it.

The mere thought of spending the rest of my life on some weird planet on the opposite side of the universe makes me want to start bawling my eyes out. But I'm desperately holding myself together so I can concentrate my energy on figuring out a way to get back to Earth.

The three robots stand outside our cell with

their laser guns, guarding the three of us. I nickname them Huey, Dewey, and Louie, just to keep things interesting.

"Your mother was a washing machine," I tell them.

They just stare at me with their penetrating red-light eyes. They've got no sense of humor. Zero. Zip. Zilch.

Of course, they're not programmed to laugh. Or speak. They do whir, but only when they twitch their heads or make jerky movements. Mostly, they just stand perfectly still and gaze at us. Like those boring statues of Loving Leader back on Earth.

An idea suddenly hits me. An escape plan.

I imitate the robot guarding me. I stand frozen, bend my arms in one direction, jerk to an abrupt stop, freeze for a few seconds, and then do it again in another direction. I even make a soft whirring sound. I keep the expression on my face vacant and empty, just like the stupid robot.

The robot tilts its head at me. It looks confused. I mimic its moves—pretending I'm the robot's reflection in a mirror. The robot studies me. It extends its right arm to see if I'll imitate it. I copy the move. The robot shifts its torso to the left. I do the same. The robot and I are moving in sync, like mirror images.

I figure if I distract the robot long enough, I can grab its laser gun. Then I'll escape from this cell, knock out Grissom, and pilot this spaceship back to Earth.

But I'm interrupted by a big, happy laugh. I look up. Sophie Singer stands at the bars of her cell, watching me—a wide smile on her face. Her curly brown hair flows past her shoulders. It's the first time I've actually seen her face. She looks about eleven. She's spent most of the space voyage lying on her cot with her face buried in her pillow.

"Well, what do you know?" I say. "She lives."

The robot freezes again, keeping its fierce red-light eyes and laser gun pinpointed on me.

Sophie nods. "How come you're not scared?" she asks.

"Me? I'm petrified."

Drew rises from his cot. "I'm not scared," he says. "Not one little bit."

"Don't listen to him. He's full of—"

"Ideas," says Drew. "And I'm not afraid to say so."

"So, Sophie, why are you being sent to Zorquat Three?" I've been dying to know. Well, not dying exactly. I'm actually in pretty good health.

Sophie picks up a titanium spoon from the counter in her cell. "I'll show you." She steps over to the metal bars of her cell and bangs the titanium spoon against them, one at a time, creating beautiful notes. I've never heard anything like it. With a sparkle in her eyes, she uses the spoon as a mallet to play a song on the metal bars—just like a xylophone. Not that I've ever played one.

The robot guarding her cocks its head, whirs, and freezes in place.

"Wow," I say. "That's really cool."

"Well, the judge didn't exactly feel that way about me making music."

"Different and dangerous?" I ask.

"Yeah," she says. "Creative and crazy. Can I help it if my head is filled with music?"

"Well, Sophie, you don't look dangerous to me."

"Neither do you."

"Norbert may not look dangerous," says Drew,

"but his parents were abducted by the Truth Police years ago and never seen again."

"That's awful," says Sophie. Tears well up in her eyes. "I'm so sorry, Norbert."

I picture my mother and father being taken away. My eyes start misting. But I refuse to talk about my parents. "That's okay," I say. "It's not *your* fault."

Drew won't shut up. "And you should have seen Norbert stand on our teacher's desk and do his impression of Loving Leader."

"It was really nothing," I say. "I'm not danger-ous." Unless I get a hold of a laser gun. But the robot guarding me is never going to step close enough to my cell for me to grab his weapon.

"Well, you two might not be dangerous," says Drew. "But I definitely am. I have a gray belt in karate!" He leaps into a fighting position, spread-ing his feet shoulder width apart. He flings his arms every which way, tossing karate chops in the air. "Hi-ya!" he shouts. He accidentally knocks a titanium mug off the counter in our cell. It crashes to the floor with a *clang!*

The robot guarding him tilts its head. Its beady

red-light eyes flare. *Whir!* The robot aims its laser gun at Drew and fires. A thin beam of green light shoots through our cell. *Whoosh!* The titanium mug disintegrates into thin air. It's gone in a flash.

So is Drew. He's cowering under his cot. I've never seen anyone scamper under a bed so quickly. He trembles and shivers in total fear.

Sophie and I crack up. But it's not real laughter. The truth is, all three of us are terrified. We're afraid of Grissom, and the robots...

And the fate that awaits us at the Astro-Nuts prison.

Chapter 7

After a week hurtling through space, our ship finally lands on Zorquat 3. The planet looks nothing like Drew said it would.

For starters, the sky is bright blue, not gray like back home. Fluffy white clouds float in the sky. Not brown smog. There's also a bright yellow ball in the sky.

"What *is* that thing?" asks Drew.

Grissom straightens the Viking helmet on his head. "That's the sun."

Yowza. Talk about different.

This planet also has two moons, one purple and

the other orange. The orange moon is half the size of
the purple one.

The spot where we land looks like nothing I've
ever seen before. Everything is green, lush, and ver-
dant. It's really bizarre.

The ground is covered with hundreds of tall
poles covered with leaves that flutter in the breeze.
So these must be trees. How weird.

Mountains surround the trees. One mountain
rises high above the others, like a really tall sky-
scraper. A waterfall cascades from the top of the
peak, creating a cloud of mist.

The robots unload the huge metallic crates from the cargo hold of the spaceship. Then they stand guard with their laser guns. Their tiny red eyes flicker.

Grissom marches us to Astro-Nuts Camp—a green meadow circled by primitive bungalows and funky, old-fashioned buildings. They're made from logs, Grissom tells us. Flower boxes line the bottom of every window. Having spent my entire life in a gray world, I've never seen so many outrageous colors at once. It makes my head spin. Drew and Sophie look a little dizzy too.

In the middle of the meadow stands a tall wooden flagpole. The tattered flag is bright red. I figure the color is some sort of political statement.

A siren blares. Hundreds of scruffy kids of all shapes and sizes race out of the cabins. Doors slam behind them.

I can't believe my eyes. All the inmates are wearing brightly colored clothes. None of them wear gray jumpsuits. Not one. I've never seen anything like this. I see all sorts of clothes that are banned on

Earth. Baggy pants. Short pants. Jeans. Sundresses. T-shirts. Hoodies. Flip-flops. There's even one kid in a vest and a bow tie. I'm in total shock.

The inmates gape at us and gather around the flagpole, lining up like a ragtag army. What on earth have I gotten myself into? Oops, I forgot. This isn't Earth at all.

"Greetings, Astro-Nuts!" says Grissom.

The other kids immediately raise their right hand in the air, saluting Grissom by holding up their index finger to make the number one. Strange.

A tall, bald guy wearing dark sunglasses steps out of a nearby cabin. He's got a thick black mustache and wears a shiny silver whistle on a lanyard around his neck.

Grissom turns to the three of us. "That's Warden Buckner," he whispers. "Commandant of Astro-Nuts Camp."

A chubby kid in a military jacket with a chest full of medals tags along after the warden. I'm guessing he's around seventeen.

"Who's that?" asks Sophie.

"Sergeant Sergeant," whispers Grissom. "And yes, that's his real name."

Warden Buckner and his sidekick stand at attention next to the flagpole. They look us over. The warden removes his sunglasses. His blue eyes sparkle. "You three have been deemed freaks. Oddballs. Weirdos. Nutjobs. Crackpots." He pauses.

The other kids go wild. They hoot and cheer, jump up and down, and give one another high fives. Until Warden Buckner blows his silver whistle. Then the kids immediately clam up.

"Sergeant Sergeant will now assign our three new Astro-Nuts to their units."

Sergeant Sergeant consults his Truthcorder—a handheld computer tablet. Sort of like a portable TruthScreen, only smaller.

"Drew Weaver, Nonperson Number FQ775X-9," he announces.

Drew steps forward and stands at attention.

"You'll be bunking in Boys Unit Sixteen," says Sergeant Sergeant. "Sophie Singer, Nonperson Number PB328R-7."

Sophie curtsies and steps forward to join Drew.

"Girls Unit Three," he says. "Norbert Riddle, Nonperson Number L4LUZR-1."

I can't resist cracking a joke. After all, I've got a captive audience. Literally. I wave both my hands in the air and spin around. "Yes, sir! Reporting for captivity, sir!"

The other kids snicker.

Sergeant Sergeant taps his Truthcorder. "After what happened to your parents, I'm surprised you weren't more careful. A lot more careful."

How could he possibly know about my parents? I get the strange feeling that maybe Sergeant Sergeant works for the Truth Police.

"I've definitely got my eyes on you, Norbert Riddle, Nonperson Number L4LUZR-1," he says. "You'll be in Boys Unit Sixteen."

I salute him to get more laughs. "Thanks, Sarge."

The other kids gasp.

Sergeant Sergeant narrows his eyes at me. "Never address me as Sarge. Do I make myself understood?"

I wipe the smirk off my face. "Yes, sir, Sergeant Sergeant." I salute again.

Warden Buckner blows his silver whistle. All the other kids scatter in different directions, racing back to their cabins. Doors slam shut, one after another. *Bang! Bam! Boom!* Warden Buckner and Sergeant Sergeant vanish.

Sophie, Drew, and I stand huddled together at the flagpole in the middle of the meadow—with no idea what we're supposed to do next.

Our shadows on the ground are suddenly eclipsed

by the shadows of two enormous creatures with sharp horns on their heads.

I get the horrible feeling that turning around to look is a very bad idea. I scrunch my eyes closed, convinced some hideous creature is about to pick me up and devour me in one quick gulp.

Chapter 8

gather all my courage, turn around, and look up. Grissom and a large woman tower over us. They both wear Viking helmets with sharp horns. Phew, what a relief. Grissom folds his arms across his chest. "New Astro-Nuts, meet Large Marge, head girls' counselor."

Large Marge runs her fingers through her frizzy blond hair. "Welcome to the nuthouse," she says.

"Why are both of you wearing Viking helmets?" asks Drew.

"That's our little secret," says Large Marge. "C'mon, Sophie, I'll bring you to Girls Unit Three."

Sophie gulps hard. "See you guys later," she says. "I hope."

As Grissom escorts Drew and me to Boys Unit 16, we pass a timber watchtower. Sergeant Sergeant stands in the window up top, adjusting a pair of high-powered binoculars perched on a tripod. He peers down at us and sneers.

"I'd watch out for that snoop if I were you," says Grissom. He pulls open the door to unit 16. "Welcome to your new home, boys."

Drew and I step inside the rustic barracks. The first thing I notice? No TruthScreens. Anywhere. Does this mean I can say and do whatever I want? Or are they hidden somewhere?

The door slams shut behind us. Grissom is gone.

Boys swing from the rafters and jump up and down on the bunk beds—like monkeys. They hoot and holler with hysteria.

Drew's mouth drops open. Mine does too. These guys are crazy. I mean certified nuts. Maybe some mad scientist turned a bunch of monkeys into boys.

How do I get out of this terrifying place?

A man with a ponytail and a scraggly beard gets

up from his bottom bunk bed. "Howdy there, part-ners!" he says, tipping his cowboy hat. He wears a black vest and snakeskin boots. "I'm your counselor. Name's Tex Swayzee."

"We call him Crazy Swayzee!" shouts one of the boys swinging from the rafters. He jumps down to the floor. He's got red hair and a face full of freckles. A fancy camera dangles around his neck. He snaps off a bunch of photos of Drew and me standing there in total shock.

"Let me introduce you new kids to the fellas," says Swayzee. "This here's Howie Rubenstein."

"Don't mind Howie," says a tall boy with spiked black hair. He dusts off the lapel of his tweed blazer. He wears an ascot. It's like a scarf, but worn like a tie. "He's like the paparazzi. I'm the real talent around here. Payne's the name. Roger Payne. Actor extraordinaire." He raises his hand with a dramatic flourish and in a bogus British accent recites: "'This above all: to thine own self be true.'" He turns to me. "That's a line from *Romeo and Juliet*. I'm an expert on Shakespeare."

Swayzee smiles and says. "Uh, Roger, I'm pretty sure that's from *Hamlet*."

"I knew that," says Roger. "I was just testing everyone."

What a phony baloney.

"Where do we sleep?" I ask.

A kid with impeccable taste in clothes steps forward. His argyle socks match his bow tie and V-neck sweater-vest. "There's an empty bunk under mine," he says. "Forgive me, I neglected to introduce myself. Farley Chung at your service."

"Dibs," calls out Drew. He flops himself on the bed.

Swayzee turns to me. "Well, Norbert, I reckon you can bunk over yonder." He points to the bottom bunk bed in the corner by the window.

A geeky kid with weird-looking binocular eyeglasses sits with his legs crossed on the top bunk. He's using tiny precision screwdrivers and needle-nose pliers to fine-tune some sort of high-tech gizmo.

"That there's Dominic Garcia, our resident techno-genius," says Swayzee. "He mostly keeps to himself. No one really talks to him much, because no one understands what in tarnation he says. Dominic, say hello to our new inmates."

Dominic looks up from his gizmo. "Yo, wussup, newbies?"

"See what I mean?" says Swayzee. "Complete mumbo jumbo. We think it's some dead language from an ancient civilization on Earth."

I sit down on my bunk. The springs squeak. The green blanket feels scratchy and the pillow is kind of mushy. I bounce my butt on the mattress. It's saggy and lumpy. The mattress, not my butt.

"So, what makes you two clowns different?" asks

Roger Payne. He throws his head back and looks down his nose. "You guys don't look dangerous to me."

"I'm not different or dangerous," I insist.

"Oh yeah? Then what are you doing on Zorquat Three with all us Astro-Nuts?"

"There's been a really big mistake. I shouldn't be here at all. I need to be sent back home right away. I'm the same as everyone else."

"Yeah, the same as everyone else *here*. Which definitely makes you different."

In other words, I stand out because I fit in.

How is that even possible?

Chapter 9

'm lying in my bunk bed late at night. Everyone in my cabin is fast asleep. It's completely dark, but I can't sleep. Not with this mushy pillow, scratchy blanket, and lumpy mattress.

Besides, I can't turn off my brain. I seriously miss dreary Aunt Martha and dreary Uncle Hank. I miss their dreary little house on Dreary Lane. I even miss mean old Mrs. Hurlbutt and Middle School Number 1022. Most of all, I miss my parents.

Outside my window the leaves on the trees rustle in the breeze. Trees sure are noisy.

The light from the two moons illuminates the

spaceship standing on its spider legs just beyond the meadow. I get an idea. A crazy idea.

Very slowly I ease out of bed, making sure the springs don't make too much noise.

I pick up my shoes from the floor and tiptoe across the room. Roger Payne suddenly rolls over. I freeze in my tracks. Then he starts snoring. I tiptoe to the rhythm of his snores. Finally I get to the door. I step outside and carefully close the door, making sure it doesn't slam shut.

I put on my shoes, slink past the flagpole, and crawl on my hands and knees across the meadow so no one will see me in the double moonlight. I head for the trees, hiding behind one, then another, as I move toward the spaceship. My plan is simple. I'm going to quietly climb up that ladder, sneak aboard the ship, and hide in the empty cargo hold. Grissom will take me back to Earth. Without ever knowing it.

Suddenly I hear noises. I duck behind the thick trunk of a big tree.

Grissom, Large Marge, and the three robot guards march across the meadow toward the spaceship. They stop next to the ladder. Just my luck.

The robots stand poised, facing out in different directions, with their laser guns aimed toward the trees. Their fierce red eyes comb the woods. They know I'm out here. I'm sure of it.

Large Marge hugs Grissom. She plants a kiss on his lips. Their Viking helmets clink together.

"Drive safely," says Large Marge. "Be sure to wear your seat belt."

Now I get it. They're a thing. That explains the matching helmets.

Grissom nods and climbs the ladder to the spaceship. The robot guards follow him. The door to the spaceship closes and seals shut with a firm clank.

With a soft roar the spaceship launches into the starry night sky. Slowly at first, then—*kerpow!*—it blasts into space, shrinking to a speck in the sky.

There is now no way off this planet. It's official. I'm totally stuck here.

My heart sinks.

I wait until Large Marge leaves, then I sneak back through the trees to unit 16, careful to avoid being seen by Sergeant Sergeant and his high-powered binoculars in his watchtower. Again I wonder how

Sergeant Sergeant knows my parents went missing. Does he know where they are?

I hear whispers and grunts off in the distance. Large Marge and a group of kids, silhouetted by the double moonlight, move large metal crates into a mysterious shed that looks like a big black box. I can't get any closer without getting caught, so I keep my distance.

Suddenly a long, howling cry fills the air. I'm scared stiff. Then I see someone standing by the flagpole. I recognize the ponytail, beard, and cowboy hat. It's my counselor—Tex Swayzee. He's howling at the two moons in the sky. Now I know why they call him Crazy Swayzee.

I quietly sneak back inside my cabin and get under the blanket.

"What were you doing outside, New Kid?" asks Roger Payne suddenly. I hadn't realized that he was awake.

"Nothing," I lie.

"I know you think you don't belong here. But you seem pretty different to me," says Roger.

The thought of being different and stuck here on Zorquat 3 forever makes me incredibly homesick.

I roll over and silently cry into my mushy pillow.

Eventually I cry myself to sleep.

I find myself drifting through a big building, walking past row upon row of tall shelves, each holding racks of test tubes filled with pink powder. Each test tube is labeled with the serial number of a different nonperson. I see hundreds, thousands, millions . . . billions of test tubes. Astonished, I spin around, accidentally knocking test tubes from the shelves. They break on the floor, and pink powder flies everywhere.

What have I done?

Suddenly Loving Leader's face juts out from the

TruthScreen on the wall. He points his finger at me and shouts: "Norbert Riddle, Nonperson Number L4LUZR-1. Are you daydreaming again? Wake up."

I can't see through the clouds of pink powder!

"Wake up, Norbert! *WAKE UP!*"

Chapter 10

I open my bleary eyes. Crazy Swayzee shakes my shoulders. "Wake up!" he says. "Rise and shine, porcupine!"

This is no dream. It's the next morning, and I really am an inmate at Astro-Nuts Camp.

A horn blasts a wonky version of "Twinkle, Twinkle, Little Star" to wake everyone up. *Bwaah bwaah blooot blooot blurp blurp blooot!*

"Last one to the flagpole is a rotten egg," says Swayzee.

Roger points to me. "That'll be you, New Kid."

Everyone runs out the door. It slams shut behind us.

As we race to the flagpole, Roger sticks out his foot. I trip over it and fall facedown in the meadow. Needless to say, I'm the rotten egg.

"Well done," says Roger. Is that his idea of an egg joke? Because it's definitely rotten.

When all the inmates have assembled at the flagpole, Warden Buckner blows his silver whistle.

HEADS UP, ASTRO-NUTS. TODAY IS BACKWARD DAY OF COURSE, EVERY DAY AT ASTRO-NUTS CAMP IS BACKWARD DAY. BUT TODAY IS ESPECIALLY BACKWARD!

What is this bizzaro place? I turn to Crazy Swayzee. "What in the world is Backward Day?"

"Don't you worry none," says Crazy Swayzee. "You'll see for yourself in the mess hall."

Long tables and benches fill the mess hall. Each unit sits together at the same long table. The girls with their units. The boys with our units. I sit next to Drew. He seems as nervous as I am, but he puts on a brave face.

Today being Backward Day, for breakfast we're served dinner, starting with dessert: ice cream sundaes. I've never seen an ice cream sundae before. I have no idea what this strange thing is. Swayzee says it's a bowl of vanilla ice cream covered with chocolate syrup, nuts, whipped cream—and topped with a bright-red cherry. Everyone else chows it down with big smiles on their faces, so I figure, what the heck, I'll give it a try.

Wow! This sure beats Aunt Martha's gruel.

Next comes the main course: spaghetti and meatballs. For breakfast! I'm totally flabbergasted. This is utterly insane. But I have to admit, the spaghetti and meatballs sure taste great. Breakfast will never be the same again.

I hold up a meatball on the end of my fork. "So, speaking of meatballs, how often does Grissom bring more kids like us in his spaceship?"

"Once every six months," says Swayzee.

Six months!

I can't handle this crazy place for six months! I need to go home now!

When everyone finishes eating, Warden Buckner blows his whistle. "Since today is Backward Day, it's now time for grace before the meal."

Swayzee turns to face our table, removes his cowboy hat, and places it over his heart. He bows his head and closes his eyes. "I just wanna thank the universe for a thing or two, like our new bunkmates—Norbert and Drew."

Roger Payne looks up toward the ceiling. "Thanks for the meal I'm about to swallow and for making me a tough act to follow."

Farley Chung straightens his argyle bow tie. "Thank you for our daily bread and also for the lovely threads."

I have no idea why everyone mumbles something different. "What's wrong with you guys? Can't everyone say the same thing? Like the Pledge of Subservience?"

Swayzee tosses his cowboy hat back on his head. "Here at Astro-Nuts Camp, you can say whatever grace you feel like saying."

"To Loving Leader?" I ask.

"No, silly, to a higher power," says Swayzee.

"You mean there's someone more powerful than Loving Leader?"

Dominic Garcia stops adjusting his gizmo with a precision screwdriver. "You can believe whatever you want to believe."

Everyone turns to me. I get the impression they're all expecting me to bow my head and say something profound. The pressure is on. Peer pressure, that is. "Listen, I hate to be a party pooper, but I really haven't got a prayer."

Roger laughs. "You can say that again."

I suddenly feel a big hand on my shoulder. I nearly hit the ceiling.

"Good morning, boys." Warden Buckner stands

behind me with one hand on my shoulder and his other hand on Drew's shoulder. "I trust you enjoyed breakfast."

Sergeant Sergeant dodders behind the warden, tapping the screen of his Truthcorder. Feverishly. Like he's documenting everything I'm doing. Sergeant Sergeant leans back against a wall and, still staring at his Truthcorder, mutters, "You're in deep trouble now."

Sophie stands beside Sergeant Sergeant. She flashes me a timid grin.

Warden Buckner clears his throat. "This morning I'm going to give our new inmates—Norbert, Drew, and Sophie..."

I gulp hard, expecting the worst.

He continues, "...a tour of Astro-Nuts Camp."

I breathe a sigh of relief.

"But before we get started, Farley, would you kindly take our three new inmates to wardrobe?"

Farley nods. "I thought you'd never ask."

I gather my courage and raise my hand. "Excuse me, Warden Buckner...."

The warden laughs. "There's no need to raise your hand, Norbert. And please, call me Bucky."

"Okay, uh, Bucky, listen, I'd love to stick around to find out what's for lunch, but I really have to get back to Earth."

"We can't send you back, Norbert. We can't send anyone back. I suggest you accept the fact you're here to stay."

"Please, Bucky, there must be some way off this planet."

"Well, yes, there is. If you refuse to participate in camp activities, we'll send you somewhere else."

At last, a glimmer of hope. "Really?" I ask. "Where?"

Bucky holds up three fingers. "Three strikes and you'll be sent to a barren asteroid to break boulders with a sledgehammer for the rest of your life. With no way off. Ever."

I cringe and tremble, terrified at the thought. That's not exactly happily ever after. Not by a long shot. Bucky walks away.

I turn to Drew and Sophie. "But how will I ever find my parents?"

Still leaning against the wall, his attention focused on his Truthcorder, Sergeant Sergeant taps the screen, pumps his fist, and mumbles, "I know exactly where they're hidden, and no one will ever figure it out."

"Huh?" I look to Sergeant Sergeant. "Where are they? Please, you've gotta tell me!"

Sergeant Sergeant shakes his head. "Sorry, Nonperson Number L4LUZR-1. That's for me to know and you to find out.' He cackles a sinister laugh and scurries away.

Cruel, right?

Chapter 11

Farley Chung fumbles with a key to open the green door of a huge bungalow.

Standing next to me on the steps, Sophie whispers in my ear. "How does Sergeant Sergeant know where your parents are?"

"That's what I'd like to know."

Drew keeps his voice low. "I bet he's got all of our permanent records on that Truthcorder. You have to get ahold of that thing."

"And how am I supposed to do that?"

"We'll help you," says Sophie. Her eyes light up.

"Why would you guys ever want to help me?"

Sophie smiles. "Because you're sweet and you make us laugh. Right, Drew?"

Drew looks to me and rolls his eyes. "Yeah, what she said. Besides, I've always wanted to see my permanent record."

Farley flings the door open and beckons us to step inside the dark building. He flips on the lights. The room is overstuffed with racks upon racks of colorful clothes. "We've got everything you ever imagined. Checkered pants! Paisley shirts! Satin evening gowns!"

He flips another switch. More lights brighten the hall, revealing endless shelves of garments and accessories. He throws yet another lever, illuminating display tables of shoes and assorted footwear.

Our mouths drop open. The three of us have never seen anything like this. We've been relegated to wearing gray jumpsuits and black military boots our entire lives. We've never been allowed to choose our own clothes. Loving Leader made the decision for us.

Farley frolics through the massive storeroom, skipping from rack to rack. He holds up a turquoise sequined jacket. "We have any clothes your heart desires!"

He waves a black lace dress. "Take anything you want." He brandishes a blue denim vest. "Don't be shy! Try on whatever you like." He picks up a tartan scarf and tosses it around his neck. "Changing rooms are right over there."

I honestly don't know where to look first. The tremendous assortment of clothes is overwhelming!

Sophie raises her hand. "Uh, how do we decide what clothes we want to wear?"

"Dress to express," says Farley. "Express your personality. Your uniqueness. Your individuality. Let your clothes make a statement."

I scratch my head. "But Loving Leader says individuality is an illness. Uniqueness threatens our way of life. Originality is pure evil...."

"At Astro-Nuts Camp you're free to think for yourself," says Farley. "I don't know about you, but I'm going to find a new argyle sweater. Something in cashmere. Or possibly alpaca." He strides down the aisle toward shelves piled high with handwoven sweaters of every color and design.

Drew starts combing through a rack of fleece jackets. I stand by his side, pretending fleece jackets fascinate me.

"How do we get hold of Sergeant Sergeant's Truthcorder?" I ask.

"Leave it to me." Drew removes a camouflage jacket from its wooden hanger and tries it on. "What do you think?"

"We just can't get caught."

"No, I mean what do you think of this jacket?"

I think it looks ridiculous, but I don't want to insult Drew. "Now that's a jacket," I say. I'm just stating a fact. Drew takes it as a compliment.

Sophie whirls toward us wearing bright-yellow overalls, a blue-and-green-striped shirt, and silver sparkle shoes. She proudly spins in her new outfit. "Isn't this just adorable?"

Drew's mouth drops open. "Wow, you look incredibly...different."

Sophie blushes. "Norbert, what are you going to wear?"

NO DRESS CODE?

"Nothing."

Sophie raises her eyebrows. "Well, you'll definitely make a unique fashion statement."

I tug at the collar of my gray jumpsuit. "I mean, I'm going to stick with this."

"Why?" asks Drew.

"To prove I'm not different. That I'm a conformist

like everyone else on Earth. So Bucky will send me home."

Farley grins. "Yeah, but here at Astro-Nuts Camp, wearing a gray jumpsuit makes you stick out like a sore thumb. Which makes you a nonconformist."

I smile. "We'll just see about that."

Chapter 12

As Bucky promised (or threatened, depending on your point of view), he takes Drew, Sophie, and me on a tour of the entire Astro-Nuts Camp.

Sergeant Sergeant tags along with us, clutching his Truthcorder close to his chest.

I shoot a knowing glance at Drew. He nods with a smirk on his face. We're definitely going to get our mitts on that thing so I can get a glimpse of my permanent record and find out where my parents are.

Bucky stares at my gray jumpsuit. "Bold wardrobe choice," he says.

"See, I'm not different. I belong back on Earth."

"Nice try, Norbert. But you could have picked out any clothes you wanted. Refusing to express your uniqueness doesn't prove you're normal. It proves you're refusing to participate."

"But this is who I really am. Honest."

Bucky sighs. "Suit yourself. But I'm afraid this is strike one."

Okay, this is bad. But not terrible. I've still got two strikes to go before I m banished to a barren asteroid. I'm not worried. Much. I'm sure I'll be able to convince Bucky I'm normal before I get strike two. I hope.

The first stop on our tour is an old-fashioned timber cottage.

Wild music with a funky beat fills the main room. A bunch of kids stand in a circle on the shiny oak floor.

I spot that show-off Roger standing alongside other kids in the circle. He puts his thumbs in his ears, wiggles his fingers, crosses his eyes, and then sticks out his tongue at me. Roger is a talented guy.

Drew, Sophie, and I have no idea what's going to happen. We watch from the sidelines as Roger steps into the center of the circle.

"I love to dance!" he yells. With his feet apart, he starts dancing like a monkey. He bends his knees and bops up and down. He raises his left hand above his head, picks an imaginary banana, and then picks another with his right hand. He keeps plucking make-believe bananas. Then he scratches make-believe fleas.

The kids around the circle imitate Roger, all dancing like monkeys. I've heard of "Monkey see, monkey do," but this is ridiculous.

I'm stunned. "They've all gone completely bananas. No pun intended."

"Yeah, they really need to stop monkeying around," says Drew.

Sophie snaps her fingers to the beat. "I love the music. But whoa! These kids are going ape."

Sergeant Sergeant looks up from his Truthcorder and stops tapping the screen for a brief moment. He's been eavesdropping on our conversation—of course. "They don't call this place Astro-Nuts for nothing," he says.

Roger points to one of the girls dancing like a

monkey. He returns to the circle, and the girl steps into the center.

"I love to dance!" she yells, just like Roger did. She places her left hand on her hip, throws her right hand in the air, points her index finger toward the ceiling, and wiggles her hips four times. Then she puts her right hand on her hip, raises her left index finger in the air, and wiggles her hips again. The other kids imitate her dance moves and start adding funky variations. One girl grabs her ankle and jerks her body all around.

Drew bops his head enthusiastically. "Astro-Nuts really know how to wiggle their butts!"

The next stop on Bucky's tour turns out to be a big wooden bungalow.

Inside we discover kids hurling balloons filled with different-colored paints at canvas sheets hung on the walls. *Splat! Splort! Sploosh!* The balloons explode, splashing and spattering bursts of purple, yellow, green, orange blue, and red paint all over the place! The paint drips everywhere.

"What a mess!" says Sophie.

MAKING A SPLASH !

Seeing all the paint flying everywhere suddenly makes me sad. I feel like I'm about to cry.

"What's the matter, Norbert?" asks Sophie. "Are you okay?"

I pull myself together. "Sorry, this just reminds me of my mother. She was an artist. I remember she threw paint at walls too."

"Oh, this is nothing!" says Drew. "I used to

throw paint at walls all the time. One time I threw a whole bunch of paint at walls in our house. My parents thought I had lost my mind. But the walls looked really cool. The floors? Not so much."

"You're all free to join in if you want," offers Bucky.

"Don't mind if I do," says Sergeant Sergeant. He places his Truthcorder on a nearby shelf for safe-keeping and joins the mayhem.

"Sure," says Drew. "Why not?" He winks at me.

Drew flings a red balloon at one wall. He throws a purple balloon at another wall. Then he pitches a blue balloon—*whoops!*—right at Sergeant Sergeant's nose. It pops, covering his face with blue paint.

"Help!" yells Sergeant Sergeant. "I can't see!" He stumbles around the room, thrashing about and waving his hands in all directions.

Bucky Buckner blows his silver whistle and races over to help his assistant. All the kids stop throwing balloons. They gather around Sergeant Sergeant.

Drew gives Sophie and me the thumbs-up sign—secretly. Then he pushes his way through the crowd.

"I'm so sorry, Sergeant Sergeant," he says. "Are you okay? I didn't mean to hit you with a paint balloon. It was an accident. Honest. Please forgive me."

Sergeant Sergeant wipes the paint from his face. "Sure, kid," he groans. "I forgive you—this time. But trust me, I won't forget."

While everyone else is distracted by all the hullabaloo, I step over to the shelf and casually sneak a peek at the Truthcorder. Sophie stands lookout.

I touch the screen. It lights up.

Sophie harrumphs a warning. I quickly step back from the Truthcorder. I look up.

Bucky gazes at me. A miffed expression on his face.

Gulp.

Chapter 13

"**D**rew, you're welcome to stay here if you like," says Bucky.

"Cool," says Drew, grabbing another balloon.

Sergeant Sergeant grabs his Truthcorder and marches back to his watchtower to wash up and change his clothes.

Drew *wants* to stay behind in the big wooden bungalow. I'm not sure why. Maybe he really loves throwing paint balloons at walls. Or maybe he just wants Bucky to think that. Why? Maybe so Bucky won't suspect Drew threw that paint balloon in Sergeant Sergeant's face on purpose.

Bucky's tour continues without Drew. He doesn't say a word about catching me red-handed with Sergeant Sergeant's Truthcorder. Does he know what I'm looking for? Why hasn't he said anything? Will this be strike two? My mind reels. I have no idea what to expect...besides the worst.

Bucky ushers Sophie and me into another bungalow. We're standing in a large room filled with bizarre musical instruments.

Dominic Garcia uses two mallets to bang away at ten brass kettles set on a rack. *Bing! Bang! Bing! Bing! Boing!*

Farley Chung uses large sticks to clang metal bars hanging above wide tubes that cause the sound to echo. *Clink! Clonk! Clinkity! Clunk!*

Other kids thump huge conga drums, shake sticks covered with small bells, pluck strings stretched across wood frames, and bang enormous gongs. *Whumpity whump! Ring-a-ding-a-ling! Boinnng!*

Together the strange sounds create a beautiful rhapsody.

WE FACE THE MUSIC.

Howie Rubenstein roams around the room with his camera, shooting photos of this outrageous orchestra in action.

Bucky wanders over to an enormous horn bent into the shape of a coiled snake twice his size. He blows into the mouthpiece. *Brappppp! Bwoppp! Bwonkkk!*

Sophie taps me on the shoulder. "Did you see your permanent record?" she whispers. "Did you figure out where your parents are?"

I shake my head. "Sergeant Sergeant keeps his Truthcorder locked. I need the password to get in."

"Bummer." Sophie picks up a slender mallet and gently strikes a row of giant metal urns of various shapes. *Plink! Plank! Plinkity! Plonk!* "Maybe his Truthcorder is connected to a bigger computer in his watchtower," she says.

"Yeah, maybe."

That means breaking into Sergeant Sergeant's watchtower. Hmmm.

Sophie plinks the urns and starts making cool musical sounds. She really gets into it. She asks Bucky if she can stay behind to jam with the oddball orchestra.

"Sure," says Bucky.

Yikes! Now I'm totally alone with Bucky Buckner.

We walk toward the meadow. I don't say a word. Now that we're alone, is he going to ask me why I was looking at Sergeant Sergeant's Truthcorder? Am I about to sink into deeper trouble?

Bucky clears his throat. "So, Norbert, have you seen anything so far that captures your imagination?"

Now I'm really terrified. Is he alluding to the Truthcorder? Or the different activities I've seen?

In my head I see Loving Leader pointing his finger at me. "Imagination is insanity!" he yells.

Is Bucky trying to trick me into saying I'm different?

"No, nothing captures my imagination...because I have no imagination. None at all. My mind is as blank as the gray wallpaper in Aunt Martha and Uncle Hank's house. I'm totally mundane. Completely ordinary. Downright boring. I swear."

"Well, we'll have to find something for you," says Bucky.

We walk past the ominous black shed where I saw Large Marge and a group of kids carrying crates last night. A padlock holds the door shut. What could be inside that thing? Giant spiders? Hundreds of snakes? Bats? Alligators? A shark tank?

I point to the big black shed. "What's that?" I ask.

"You know, you're a very curious young man," says Bucky Buckner.

Now I'm confused. Is he complimenting my natural curiosity? Or is he talking about seeing me sneak a peek at the Truthcorder? Am I just being paranoid?

"That's the Black Box." Bucky rubs his hands

together. "I strongly suggest you stay far away from that."

"What's inside it?"

Bucky hesitates. "Something *very* different. And *very* dangerous."

No, I'm definitely not paranoid.

I'm *paralyzed*.

With the most intense fear I've ever felt in my life.

Chapter 14

During lunch in the mess hall, I spot a beautiful girl sitting with her unit at a nearby table. She's got long blond hair in a bouncy ponytail, a cute smile, and twinkly blue eyes. She's eating her macaroni and cheese with chopsticks, which strikes me as odd. She's the only person in the entire mess hall doing that. Definitely unusual. But kind of adorable.

Dominic Garcia notices me staring at her, and I ask him who she is.

"That's Charlene Gordon," says Dominic. "She eats only with chopsticks. Always. She's sort of crazy, if you ask me."

Sergeant Sergeant leans against a wall, tapping the screen of his Truthcorder. He looks up. His eyes dart back and forth. He notices me staring at Charlene. He scowls. He's watching my every move. Gathering evidence for Bucky to give me strike two. I just know it.

"So, boys, how's the tour going?" asks Swayzee. "Anything here at Astro-Nuts Camp catch your fancy?"

Drew's brand-new camouflage jacket is covered with red, orange, and green splotches of fresh paint. "I love the art room," he says. "It's a smash, if you know what I mean."

"How about you, Norbert? Why didn't you ditch the jumpsuit? Don't you want to express your individuality?"

I shrug. "I don't have any individuality to express." I'm determined to convince everyone I'm just an ordinary Joe who should be sent back home.

"Whatever you say, partner." Swayzee gives me a sly wink. "Did you see any activities you liked?"

"Nope."

"Well, you might want to find one. You definitely don't want to strike out here."

That's for sure. I take a deep breath. "Hey, what's the story on the Black Box?"

Dominic drops his precision screwdriver into his bowl of soup and looks up from his gizmo. "What black box?" he asks.

Farley elbows Dominic in the ribs.

Roger nearly chokes on his macaroni and cheese. He shoots a concerned glance at Howie.

"So why *does* Charlene Gordon eat only with chopsticks?" asks Howie.

He aims his zoom lens at the pretty girl and starts snapping pictures.

Yeah, he's trying to change the subject.

But I'm not falling for that trick. "The big black shed near the meadow with the padlock on the door. The one Large Marge and a bunch of kids moved crates into last night."

"Oh, *that* Black Box," says Swayzee. "I honestly don't know. It ain't none of my business, so I keep my head low. I suggest you do the same."

Drew smirks. "It's solitary confinement. For troublemakers. Bucky locks Astro-Naughties inside the Black Box for up to thirty days...with aliens captured from other planets. Giant green insect people with antennae and large, bulging eyes. Reptile people with scaly heads and lobster claws. Humanoids with purple skin, huge heads, and three fingers on each hand. Think too far outside the box, and you wind up inside the box."

Now I'm freaking out. I'm scared out of my wits.

Drew suddenly bursts out laughing.

That's when I realize he made up everything he just told me. "Why are you lying?" I ask.

"I'm not lying," says Drew. "I'm fabricating."

"What's the difference?"

"I'm just making up interesting stories. You know, embellishing."

"Yeah, lying through your teeth."

"It's all in good fun," he says defensively.

"Actually, Drew's totally right about the Black Box," says Roger with a crooked smile.

"I am?" Drew starts to flip out.

So do I.

Roger leans forward. "The Black Box is...well, we better not talk about it. The walls have ears."

Dominic, Farley, and Howie nod in agreement.

Swayzee turns his head to direct our attention to the guy in the uniform leaning against the wall.

Sergeant Sergeant taps the screen of his Truthcorder and peers up. His eyes lock on me.

Yeah, I think I'll definitely stay away from the Black Box.

Far away.

Chapter 15

After lunch all the inmates of Astro-Nuts Camp get free time, when we can do as we please. Interesting.

I've never heard of anything called free time before. On Earth we call it Truth Time. We get an hour to watch a show on the TruthScreen.

My favorite show? *I Love Loving Leader.*

For one hour Loving Leader drones on and on. "Be like everyone else or beware! Believe in me, not in yourself!" You get the idea. Sure, the guy with the wild white hair scares my pants off, but I also find him amusing. He doesn't mean to be funny, but the stupid things he says crack me up.

During free time I lie down on my bottom bunk, rest my head on my pillow, and start thinking about home again. The thought of being stuck here on Zorquat 3 forever makes my eyes fill with tears. Here come the waterworks.

I roll over and bury my head in the pillow so no one will see me crying. I don't want the other guys thinking I'm a wimp. Or calling me a crybaby. But they're too busy swinging from the rafters and jumping on the beds like chimpanzees to notice me anyway.

Well, not everyone.

Drew sits on his bed, doodling in a sketch pad. Someone gave him a bunch of art supplies: pencils, erasers, pens, and Conté crayons. He's as happy as a pig in mud.

Dominic sits with his legs crossed on the bunk above me, twisting needle-nose pliers to fine-tune the high-tech gizmo he's been toiling over. The guy's obsessed. A total techie geek.

All I keep thinking is how much I want to get back home, find my mother and father, and be one happy family again. I've gotta get off this dumb planet. I've just gotta convince everyone I'm totally normal. Humdrum. Lackluster. Yep, I'm just your typical dullard from Dullsville.

The bunk bed shakes. I feel Dominic jump down from the bunk above me. His red high-top sneakers go *splort* when he lands on the floor. Maybe he decided to swing from the rafters after all.

Someone taps me on the shoulder. I dry the tears from my eyes, turn my head, and look up.

It's Dominic, sitting on the edge of my bed.

"Are you okay?" he whispers. His eyeballs look huge, magnified by the thick lenses of his binocular eyeglasses.

"Fine," I lie.

"I heard you whimpering," he says. "Listen, you wanna see something gnarly?"

"Sure," I lie. I don't have a clue what "gnarly" means.

He holds up his gizmo in the palm of his hand.

"What is it?" I ask.

"A divergent gibberish transducer."

It looks like a weird block of shiny metal with doohickeys, thingamajigs, and whatchamacallits sticking out in all directions.

"Yep, that's a divergent gibberish transducer, all right." I give him a big thumbs-up.

Dominic removes the binocular eyeglasses from his face. "You have no idea what a divergent gibberish transducer is, do you?"

"None whatsoever."

He holds his hand to his face and whispers. "Don't tell anyone, but with this puppy I can transmit messages anywhere in the universe."

Suddenly I'm very interested. "Really?" I ask.

Dominic nods. He touches his finger to his lips and then beckons me with that same finger to follow him outside.

We find a secluded spot among the trees. You know, those tall poles with leaves. Dominic tells me to talk into his divergent gibberish transducer. He says the gizmo will translate my spoken words into high-frequency neutrino impulses and transmit them across the cosmos to 526 Dreary Lane in Region 154. Instantly! Aunt Martha and Uncle Hank will receive the message as text on their TruthScreen.

"Won't Loving Leader get the message too?" I ask.

"Loving Leader never gets the message." Dominic laughs at his own joke. "I use this bad boy twenty-four/seven to text my homeys."

I throw caution to the wind. Even though there's really no wind at the moment. I speak into the gizmo in the palm of Dominic's hand.

"Hello, Aunt Martha and Uncle Hank. It's me. Norbert Riddle. I'm stuck at this crazy place on Zorquat Three, and they won't let me call you, so when you get this message, please come get me. Steal a spaceship if you have to. I hate this place. It's horrible. I miss you both very much. I even miss Aunt Martha's gruel. That's how bad this place is. No offense. I'm sorry for everything I did. But I'm not nearly as crazy as these obnoxious people. They're all certified nutjobs. Well, except my friend Dominic Garcia. He's pretty cool. But I'm begging you! Please rescue me from this crazy planet! I love you both. Love, your nephew. Norbert Riddle. P.S. I mean it! Rescue me! Now!"

Will my aunt and uncle get my urgent message? Or will Loving Leader intercept the transmission?

Chapter 16

Dominic Garcia presses a small red button. The weird gizmo wobbles in his palm. *Whoosh!* ... *Ping!*

Message sent...across the far reaches of the universe. Instantly!

"How can I ever thank you enough?" I ask.

Dominic puts his index finger to his lips. "Let's just keep this our little secret," he says.

I agree. We start moseying through the trees, heading back to the cabin. We've still got plenty of free time left.

"Can you hack your way into anything?" I ask.

"Pretty much."

"How about Sergeant Sergeant's Truthcorder, for instance?" Before Aunt Martha and Uncle Hank arrive (hopefully in a week, if they steal a spaceship right away), I need to get into my permanent record and find out where on Earth my parents are.

"That might take some doing," says Dominic. "But sure, I'd be up for the challenge. Although I definitely wouldn't want Sarge Squared to catch me doing that."

"Sarge Squared?"

"Yeah, Sergeant Sergeant. I call him Sarge Squared, but not to his face. It's my own little math joke. You know, a number multiplied by itself. Plus, he's a total square."

"Is his Truthcorder linked to some sort of supercomputer up there?" I point to the watchtower.

"Possibly," Dominic says, looking up. "Hard to say without seeing what's inside."

"You want to sneak up with me and take a look?"

"No, no, no. Definitely not. I don't mess with Sarge Squared. I don't trust the guy at all. It's one thing to hack into his Truthcorder, but it's entirely another thing completely to go in and search his quarters."

When Dominic and I step back inside the cabin, all the other kids are standing around Drew's bunk. We join the crowd, peering over their shoulders.

"What's going on?" I ask.

Roger holds up a page torn from Drew's sketch pad. "Take a look at this," he says. "It looks exactly like me." On the large piece of white paper is a caricature of Roger, with a pointy nose, stars in his eyes, and his hair arranged in huge spikes. "I sure am a handsome devil!"

"Well, he's half right about that." Tex Swayzee sits in a chair in front of Drew, posing for his portrait. Everyone's watching with bated breath. Whatever that means.

Other kids hold their caricatures. The drawing of Farley Chung has a big nose and a huge argyle smile to match his argyle socks, argyle bow tie, and argyle sweater. Howie Rubenstein, depicted with big ears and wild red hair, holds a gigantic camera in one hand and hangs from the rafters with the other.

Drew rips the finished drawing from his sketch pad and hands it to Swayzee.

"There's no slack in your rope," says Swayzee. "We've got ourselves a regular Michelangelo da Vinci." The caricature shows Crazy Swayzee with a bulbous nose, squinty eyes, and a scruffy beard—all under a huge cowboy hat. His giant head sits on top of two tiny snakeskin boots. "I can't wait to show this to everyone tonight at the Love Fest."

Love Fest? On Earth a Love Fest is a massive rally we're all forced to attend to demonstrate our love for Loving Leader—with cheers, banners, and lots of hoopla. I'm curious to see what a Love Fest is like here on Zorquat 3.

Drew flips through his sketch pad and holds up a caricature of Loving Leader with wild white hair and his hands flailing madly. I crack up. Drew turns the pages to show me his other cartoonish caricatures. There's Bucky Buckner with an enormous bald head, huge black mustache, and dark sunglasses. Sergeant Sergeant has a small, round head sinking into his military jacket, covered with a zillion medals.

"Wow. You really are the fastest draw in the west. Not to mention east, north, and south."

He smiles. "Thanks, Norbert. Listen, I don't know how to tell you this, but I've got a confession to make."

"Let me guess. The Powder Room doesn't exist. You made the whole thing up."

"Well, yes, but I was right about the Black Box, so I might be right about the Powder Room too. Anyway, that's not what I wanted to tell you." He lowers his voice. "Remember when the Truth Police threw me in prison with you?"

"Can't we forget about all that?"

"I blamed you for making me laugh in class."

"I'm really sorry about that. I should never have jumped up on Mrs. Hurlbutt's desk."

"Well, to be honest, the Truth Police didn't arrest me for laughing at your impression of Loving Leader."

I don't get it. "Then why'd they arrest you?"

Drew hesitates. "After they dragged you from the classroom, they searched my desk and found my caricatures of…"

"Mrs. Hurlbutt?" I can just picture his drawing of that nasty old biddy as a shriveled prune.

"No, not Mrs. Hurlbutt" says Drew. "Loving Leader."

Whoa. That's serious stuff. Of course, Drew could be lying again. Oops. I mean embellishing. I look into his eyes. No, he's dead serious.

"I'm sorry I blamed you for everything," says Drew. "It's my fault I'm here. Not yours. You do make me laugh, though. How can I make it up to you?"

"You don't owe me a thing."

"No, really. I'll do anything you want. Just name it."

I look out the window and catch a glimpse of the tall watchtower in the distance. "Let me think about that," I say. "I'm sure I can come up with something."

Chapter 17

I t's still Backward Day, so for dinner we eat breakfast. Yeah, pretty weird. But I have to admit, there's something funny about having scrambled eggs, cornflakes, and toast for dinner. It's so ridiculous you can't help but laugh. Well, it makes me laugh, anyway.

Tonight during the Love Fest I'm going to put my plan into action. I hope it works. It's just gotta work.

I have to find out where on Earth my parents are before Aunt Martha and Uncle Hank get here to take me back home. Traveling at super-duper-hyper-turbo-zippo-speed, they could be here in a week, which on

Zorquat 3 is eight days. That's because one day on Zorquat 3 is only twenty-one hours long—instead of twenty-four. So eight days here equals seven days on Earth. Trust me. Dominic Garcia did the math.

I'm waiting in the meadow. Just sitting on the grass. Short green vegetation that covers the ground. I'm jittery. Worried if my plan will go smoothly. Without any hiccups. I hate when I get hiccups. Of course, I'd much rather get hiccups than strike two.

The bright yellow ball in the sky slowly sinks behind the mountains. The blue sky turns green. The white clouds glow orange and red. I've never seen anything so wildly colorful. Except maybe earlier today when all those kids threw paint balloons at the walls.

Drew and Sophie join me. Not that I need to be glued back together. I just mean they come sit with me in the meadow. We watch the sky turn black. The large purple moon hangs high in the sky above us as the smaller orange moon floats nearby. Stars fill the inky darkness. They twinkle like diamonds. I've never actually seen a diamond, but that's what the song says. They look kind of cool, actually.

Back home when night falls, the gray sky turns muddy brown, then solid black. We learn about the stars in Middle School Number 1022, but we see them only on the TruthScreen. Never in the sky.

"They're so beautiful," says Sophie.

But a sad reminder that we're totally stranded on the other side of the cosmos.

"Yeah," says Drew. "We must be a zillion light-years from home."

I glare at him.

"Okay, okay," says Drew. "We're only one thousand three hundred forty-seven light-years from Earth, if you want to know the truth."

"I wonder which one is Earth," says Sophie.

I point to the tiniest dot in the sky. "Probably that one."

The sound of banging drums travels through the woods, calling everyone to the Love Fest.

We head to the outdoor amphitheater. Deep in the woods, tiers of wooden benches surround a pit. Hundreds of kids sit on the benches, bursting with excitement. You can feel the buzz in the air. Drew, Sophie, and I find a spot to sit together.

Down in the pit, Crazy Swayzee swings a huge ax, chopping fallen tree trunks into logs. Roger and Howie stack the biggest logs in the center of the pit while Sergeant Sergeant bosses them around. And of course he's still clutching his Truthcorder close to his chest, rattling his medals. So predictable. I wonder if he'll be scanning the crowd, looking for non-participation.

Other kids hurl branches, crates, and wooden school desks and chairs on top of the logs, creating a huge tower.

No one has any trouble tossing heavy objects on top of the tower. It's a cinch, really. That's because Zorquat 3 has 25 percent less gravity than Earth. So everything weighs 25 percent less here than it does on Earth.

If you weigh one hundred pounds on Earth, you weigh seventy-five pounds here on Zorquat 3. Yep, everyone gets 25 percent off. Large Marge says that fact alone makes her giddy with happiness.

The wood tower keeps growing taller and taller. It teeters and sways. The crazy thing looks like it's going to topple over any minute.

THE LEANING TOWER OF ASTRO-NUTS CAMP

Crazy Swayzee leaves his ax wedged in a log and picks up a twenty-liter metal canister. He circles the wood tower, pouring zapolyne rocket fuel all over the big logs at the bottom. Then he pours a trail of zapolyne along the ground and out from the tower in a spiral, creating a long, swirling fuse.

The crowd in the amphitheater is now delirious with anticipation. They clap their hands, stomp their feet, and chant, "Love Fest! Love Fest! Everybody do your best!" They're going absolutely hog wild. Not that I've ever seen a hog, never mind a hog going wild.

Astounded, I turn to Drew and Sophie. "These kids really are Astro-Nuts. And by 'Astro-Nuts,' I mean Astro-*Nutjobs*."

Drew and Sophie nod in agreement. I catch a glimpse of a beautiful girl sitting across the way with long blond hair. The one who eats only with chopsticks.

Suddenly all the kids in the amphitheater stand up, cheering and clapping the whole time. I lose sight of Charlene Gordon. Everyone raises their right hand in the air and holds up one finger to make the letter *I*.

They start chanting, "Insanity! Insanity! Gives you personality!"

They jump up and down in a frenzy, thrusting their right index fingers in the air. "Insanity! Insanity! Gives you personality!" they shout. "Insanity! Insanity! Embrace your humanity!"

I've got a feeling the Love Fest is about to take insanity to a whole new level.

Chapter 18

Down in the pit, Dominic Garcia hands Swayzee a LaserTorch.

Swayzee tips his cowboy hat, holds up the long, loopy gadget, and clicks the trigger. The tip of the LaserTorch lights up neon blue. He raises it high in the air.

The kids in the amphitheater go wild, hooting and hollering. "Love Fest!" they chant. "Love Fest! Everybody do your best!"

Beyond the wooden tower, a group of musicians sit with their absurd instruments. Farley Chung stands up, twirls his big mallet, and bangs an enormous gong. *Brrrronnnggggg!*

Swayzee touches the neon-blue tip of the Laser-Torch to the end of the trail of zapolyne on the ground. The small puddle of zapolyne bursts into a bright orange flame. The musicians start banging, clanking, blowing, and thumping their instruments. *Bing! Boing! Clonk! Clunk! Whumpity whump! Ring-a-ding-a-ling!*

Sophie bops her head to the melody. She points to a woman with brown pigtails clanking kettle gongs. "That's my counselor," she says. "Kitty Carpenter. She's really nice but kind of kooky." Of course, that describes almost everyone here at Astro-Nuts Camp.

"Love Fest! Love Fest! Put your spirit to the test!" Throngs of kids thrust their clenched fists in the air.

I notice Bucky Buckner sitting with the musicians. He blows into the mouthpiece of the huge horn bent into the shape of a coiled snake. *Bwop! Bwop! Bwonk!*

"Love Fest! Love Fest! Never let the real you rest!"

The bright orange flame follows the trail of zapolyne. It circles the teetering tower.

Howie Rubenstein races around the tower with his camera, snapping photos as the orange flame whizzes around the spiral of zapolyne.

Suddenly the small ball of flame hurtles into the stack of firewood.

Ba-voom!

The tower explodes into a massive fireball! And then it transforms into a towering bonfire with orange flames licking high up into the dark, star-filled sky.

Everyone's cheering like mad. Even me. The excitement is contagious.

"Love Fest!" shouts Drew, thrusting his clenched fists in the air.

Sophie giggles with glee.

I start laughing too. I hate to admit it, but I'm actually having fun.

Howie darts through the crowd, snapping tons of photos of the bonfire, the musicians beating their funky kettles and chimes, and the Astro-Nuts going nuts.

Swayzee picks up a lopsided electric guitar called a Wazooper, straps it around his neck, and steps up to a microphone. He looks up to the sky and howls at the two moons like a total madman. Then he starts strumming those eleven Wazooper strings. The band of musicians join in, plinking their gongs and chimes. Everyone starts clapping their hands to the beat.

Swayzee starts singing a crazy song.

> *"You gotta be sane to be crazy!*
> *You gotta work hard to be lazy!*
> *You gotta see clear to be hazy!*
> *Yeah, you gotta be sane to be crazy!"*

Suddenly everyone joins in, singing the lyrics with zest. I'm blown away. I mean, I've never seen anything this cool and awesome. Drew says he hasn't either. Neither has Sophie.

When the song ends, everyone howls at the moon. Even Sergeant Sergeant!

Swayzee immediately launches into another song.

E'RE NUTTY, NUTTY ASTRO-NUTS,
E'RE NUTTY AS CAN BE!
'RE NUTTY, NUTTY ASTRO-NUTS,
NO ONE'S NUTTIER THAN WE!

They're all waving their right hands in the air, pointing their index fingers to the sky.

Time to put our plan into action.

I nudge Sophie with my elbow. "Ready?" I whisper.

She nods and taps Drew on the shoulder. He's pumping his fists in the air and singing his heart out.

I get the feeling he really doesn't want to leave the Love Fest.

But he nods too. Reluctantly.

Here goes nothing.

Chapter 19

W e can't draw any attention to ourselves. We have to sneak out of here unnoticed.

I make eye contact with Dominic down in the pit. Trembling with nervous energy, I touch the tip of my nose with my index finger.

Dominic responds by scratching the back of his head. Just like we planned, he steps over to Sergeant Sergeant, whispers something in his ear, and points to the enormous gong.

Farley Chung holds up his big mallet, offering Sarge the chance to bang the huge metal disk.

It's an offer Sergeant Sergeant can't resist.

As Sarge makes his way toward the gong, Sophie, Drew, and I scrunch down low and carefully slink through the crowd. Fortunately, everyone's attention is focused on the monstrous bonfire. The orange flames soar high into the sky. The bonfire blazes and crackles like a raging beast with a life of its own.

We wend our way through the throngs of kids leaping up and down. They're dancing, shouting, and cheering.

As Sergeant Sergeant thwacks the gigantic gong, he literally jumps for joy. What a knucklehead.

To avoid being seen, we zigzag through the trees. We go one at time, stopping to hide behind each tree we pass. Crawling on our hands and knees, we traverse the meadow, hidden by the tall grass. We sidle up to the watchtower.

No floodlights shine on the watchtower. It stands in total darkness. The moonlight of the large purple moon, combined with the moonlight of the smaller orange moon, showers the watchtower in an eerie greenish-gray mist.

Single file and without uttering a word between us, we climb up the slippery rungs of the ladder.

Straight up the side of the watchtower. Drew goes first, followed by Sophie, and—last but not least— yours truly. The brains behind the operation.

Or lack thereof.

I go last in case anyone slips and falls. This way, they'll fall on me.

I really must be crazy. Oops, don't tell Bucky Buckner I said that.

Then I realize something awful. If I get caught doing this, Bucky won't just give me strike two for leaving the Love Fest. He'll also never believe I'm normal. No matter how much I swear I'm not different. Even if I wear this gray jumpsuit until it falls to tatters. This little escapade proves I'm creative, clever, and crazy as a fox—and that I clearly belong at Astro-Nuts.

We'd better not get caught. That's all I can say.

Drew climbs onto the observation deck and then reaches down to give Sophie a helping hand. Does Drew help me up? No. I get the privilege of hoisting myself up to the deck. What a pal.

Standing at the railing, we hear singing and cheering from the Love Fest in the distance. We can even make out the tall orange flame of the bonfire. The trees cast black shadows that flutter like demons reaching out to grab us.

Drew creaks open the door atop the watchtower. He steps inside the dark room and flips a switch on the wall, and the entire watchtower lights up!

"Turn that off, you numskull!" I bark at Drew.

Sophie immediately flips the switch off. "Norbert,

there's no need to be nasty," she says. "We may be breaking and entering, but that's no excuse for bad manners."

I ease the door shut behind me. "Sorry. Please forgive me." From a pocket of my gray jumpsuit, I take out Dominic's miniature LaserLight to shed some light on the situation.

There's a pair of high-powered binoculars attached to a tripod, facing out a window. Sophie takes a peek to see what they're focused on. "Apparently, Sergeant Sergeant enjoys astronomy," she says. "He's got these things pointed directly at that purple moon. Wow, you can see all the craters."

"Yeah, but he can also aim those things straight into unit sixteen," says Drew. "Or any cabin, bungalow, or building he wants to spy on."

I sweep the LaserLight around the room. "There's nothing up here but maps of the stars and planets. No supercomputer. No secret documents. No nothing." Just a small cot, a public-address system to make announcements, a flügelhorn to blast "Twinkle, Twinkle, Little Star" every morning, and some fantastic views. The windows offer a spectacular panorama of the waterfall that tumbles from the tall mountain peak towering over Astro-Nuts Camp. A gazillion points of light shimmer in the night sky.

We hear a sudden hubbub of laughter and shouting. The watchtower rumbles. Someone's climbing up the ladder. Someone hefty, wearing clinking medals.

If I get caught up here, my life will be officially ruined. Forever.

Chapter 20

None of us want to get caught in Sergeant Sergeant's watchtower. Especially by Sergeant Sergeant!

Alarmed, we look out the windows. Throngs of kids emerge from the woods, returning to camp from the Love Fest. They laugh and shout as they walk across the meadow.

The watchtower wobbles with each step Sergeant Sergeant takes up the ladder. We have to get out of here before he reaches the observation deck and finds us standing in the windows.

Lickety-split, Drew closes the blinds to buy us a few precious seconds before Sergeant Sergeant spots us.

I turn to Sophie. "Hide!" I whisper.

I crawl under the cot.

Drew dives out an open window.

Sophie freezes, unsure where to go.

The entire watchtower trembles as Sergeant Sergeant reaches the deck.

He opens the door, flips on the light switch, and steps inside the room.

Panic-stricken, I cringe under the cot, afraid for Sophie and the wrath of Sergeant Sergeant.

Sophie stands in the center of the room, holding the flügelhorn to her lips. She blasts "Twinkle, Twinkle, Little Star." Loudly. *Bwaah bwaah blooot blooot...bwaaaaaaacng!* She hits a long sour note.

"What are you doing in here?" demands Sergeant Sergeant.

Sophie lowers the flügelhorn. "Auditioning," she says. "I understand you're the one who plays 'Twinkle, Twinkle, Little Star' every morning. I'd really like to do that too. So I thought I'd try out for you."

"Well, it sounds like you need a lot more practice. You really shouldn't be up here."

Sophie points to the high-powered binoculars. "What are those for?"

"Uh...stargazing." Sergeant Sergeant sets his Truthcorder on the desk and steps over to his high-powered binoculars. He studies them for a moment, a puzzled look on his face. Has he noticed something out of place? Did Drew put the tripod back in the wrong spot?

"Can I take a peek?"

"I guess so. Let me focus them for you." Sergeant Sergeant shrugs, turns off the light, and looks through the high-powered binoculars, aimed at the purple moon.

While Sergeant Sergeant adjusts the lenses, Sophie puts her hand behind her back and signals me, pointing to the open door.

I crawl out from under the cot. I see the Truthcorder lying on the desk in the dark. Should I reach up and grab it?

"Here you go," says Sergeant Sergeant. "The purple moon of Zorquat Three." He looks up from the binoculars to offer Sophie a turn.

I freeze in the darkness. I think I'm going to keel over.

"Oh, I was hoping to see the *orange* moon," says Sophie.

Sergeant Sergeant sighs. He grabs his Truth-corder and peers through the high-powered binoculars to readjust the focus on the other moon.

Sophie signals me again, wagging her finger behind her back.

I quickly crawl out the open door and around the deck to join Drew. I raise my head just above the window ledge to check on Sophie.

Sergeant Sergeant is still focusing his binoculars on the orange moon.

"You know, you're right," says Sophie. "I really shouldn't be up here"

"It's okay," says Sergeant Sergeant. "You can take a look."

"No, I better get back to my cabin. Thanks anyway. I'm really sorry about this. It won't happen again. Good night." She abruptly walks out the door and starts climbing down the ladder.

Sergeant Sergeant looks up from the binoculars and shrugs.

While Sophie climbs down the ladder, Drew and I quietly slip between the spaces in the deck railing.

Careful not to make a peep, we shinny down to one of the crossbeams. I feel like Howie, swinging from the rafters in our cabin.

We continue lowering ourselves, gently climbing from one crossbar to the next, until we drop safely to the ground. With 25 percent less gravity, hitting the ground doesn't hurt nearly as much as it does back home.

Except I miscalculate the distance and land on my butt. "Owwww!" I moan.

Drew claps his hand over my mouth.

Above us in the watchtower, the lights suddenly go on, illuminating the night sky. Sergeant Sergeant opens the door, steps onto the observation deck, and looks down to the ground.

This definitely won't look good on my permanent record.

Chapter 21

Directly above us, Sergeant Sergeant walks around the deck of his watchtower, scanning the turf below. He knows there's something out here. I just hope he doesn't know it's us.

In the distance Sophie scurries across the meadow to Girls Unit 3. She mixes in with the throngs of kids returning from the Love Fest. She disappears into the crowd. At least one of us got away. I'm glad it was Sophie.

Drew and I remain perfectly still, afraid to move a muscle. Fortunately, we're hidden underneath the watchtower, cloaked by the shadows.

We hear Sergeant Sergeant's footsteps high above us, creaking across the wooden deck of his watchtower. Each squeak sends a chill up my spine. I'm praying to a higher power that my stomach doesn't suddenly growl.

I shut my eyes, desperately trying not to move an inch. Concentrating all my energy on staying frozen like one of Grissom's robot guards.

Finally Sergeant Sergeant steps back into his room atop the watchtower. We hear his door creak closed and the latch click shut. We wait a few more minutes, sitting motionless in the darkness to make certain the coast is clear.

Then we scamper back to good old unit 16, darting through the trees.

We race inside the cabin. The door slams shut behind us. We catch our breath.

"Where have you two rapscallions been?" asks Crazy Swayzee.

"Uh, rehearsing," says Drew.

"Rehearsing what?" demands Swayzee.

Drew turns to me. "Go ahead, Norbert, show him."

"Show him what?"

"Your impression of Loving Leader."

"Uh, I'd rather not. That's what got me sent here in the first place."

"Well, you're here now, so what difference does it make?"

"But there's no desk to stand on."

Drew drags the steamer trunk sitting at the foot of Swayzee's bunk into the center of the cabin. "Here you go, Norbert," he says. "Use this."

All the other kids clap and cheer, urging me to do my act.

I can't believe they're actually encouraging me to make them laugh. That's a first.

I stand on top of Swayzee's trunk. All eyes are on me. The pressure is on. I muss up my hair. Howie Rubenstein grabs his camera and shoots a whole bunch of photos of me doing my impression.

"My fellow earthlings," I say. "There is no greater joy than the joy of conformity. Yes, the only way to make people happy is to get rid of unhappy people. You're free to disagree with me—if you agree to go to jail. Remember, it's a free country, but only for me. Being unique makes you a freak, and being a freak is bleak. Besides, refusing to conform is conforming to nonconformity, which is still conformity. So why not conform directly to conformity? Then everyone can be completely equal. Equally dressed. Equally fed. Equally housed. Equally oppressed. Equally dull. Equally dreary.

"Yes, my fellow earthlings, one for all, and all for me! Ask not what Loving Leader can do for you, but what you can do for Loving Leader." I hold up two fingers and my thumb to make the letter *W*. "Whatever!" I shout.

Everyone cracks up laughing. Crazy Swayzee howls.

It's nice to feel appreciated for once in my life. I love the attention, and, to be totally honest, making people laugh makes me feel like I've got some sort of superpower.

They're all doubled over in hysterics. Except Roger Payne. He eyes me with contempt and jealousy. He's giving me the willies.

Is Roger some sort of spy? Is he going to blow my cover by telling Bucky Buckner I'm not the conformist I'm pretending to be?

And what about Howie Rubenstein? He's got incriminating photos of my whole act!

Did I just seal my own fate?

What have I done?

Chapter 22

It's morning, and we're eating breakfast in the mess hall. Today is a normal Forward Day. No one actually calls it Forward Day, and a Forward Day is definitely not normal, either. Every day is abnormal. But around here that's normal. If you know what I mean.

"Is there really nothing up there?" asks Dominic as he digs into his oatmeal.

I raise my glass of orange juice. "Nope, just binoculars and maps."

That means there's only one way to find out where my parents are. I've got to get my hands on Sergeant Sergeant's Truthcorder long enough for Dominic to hack into my permanent record. All without Sergeant Sergeant noticing his Truthcorder is missing, and without getting caught. Good luck pulling that off.

"Attention, Norbert Riddle, Nonperson Number L4LUZR-1," says a deep voice.

I nearly spray the orange juice from my mouth. Speak of the devil. Sergeant Sergeant approaches our table, clutching his Truthcorder. He taps the screen a few times and then holds the device close to his chest.

Does he know we broke into his watchtower last night?

I set down my glass of orange juice. "Yes, Sergeant. By the way, sir, you don't have to be so formal. You can just call me Nonperson Number L4LUZR-1."

"All right, Mr. Smarty-Pants. When you finish breakfast, Warden Buckner wants to see you in his office, on the double."

"Me too?" asks Drew.

"Just Mr. Smarty-Pants. Is there some reason Warden Buckner should want to see you, too?"

"No," says Drew. "I just have an incredible fear of missing out."

"You won't be missing out on anything," says Sergeant Sergeant. "I can assure you of that."

Crazy Swayzee tips his cowboy hat. "I'll make sure Norbert heads over to Bucky's office straightaway. Right after he finishes his waffles."

The other guys in unit 16 give me the eye. This can't be good. Not one bit.

I get the terrible feeling Sergeant Sergeant knows we were inside his watchtower last night. I'm sure of it. He's just drawing out the suspense. I bet he went straight to Bucky last night and told him everything. And now Bucky Buckner suspects I'm the instigator.

Or maybe that's not it at all.

Maybe Bucky heard about the impression I did for the guys last night in the cabin. You know, my impersonation of Loving Leader. Yeah, maybe that's it.

I bet Roger squealed. That know-it-all probably told Bucky everything. And Howie showed Bucky all the pictures he took of me standing on Swayzee's trunk. With my hair all tousled to look like His All-Knowing Eternal Excellency. I'm dead meat.

As I walk across the meadow toward Bucky's office, I pass the dreaded Black Box.

Chills run up and down my spine.

I imagine myself being thrown into solitary confinement in the Black Box, surrounded by slimy aliens captured from other planets. Giant green insect people examine me with their large, bulging eyes and waving antennae. Reptile people snap their lobster claws in my face. Purple-skinned aliens with huge heads and three fingers on each hand touch me, making my skin crawl.

In my head I hear Drew repeating over and over: *Think too far outside the box, and you wind up inside the box.*

My heart beats like one of those crazy kettle gongs.

I walk into Bucky's office. He sits behind a big glass desk. He touches a button.

A large TruthScreen lowers from the ceiling, covering the wall behind him. It's the first TruthScreen I've seen since arriving here at Astro-Nuts Camp.

"Someone wants to speak with you," says Bucky. "You'd better sit down."

Not Loving Leader. Please not Loving Leader. My head spins. I think I'm going to faint. Or puke. Hopefully not at the same time.

Chapter 23

grip the arms of my comfy chair, holding on for dear life.

Bucky presses another button on his desk. The TruthScreen lights up.

I sink my head into my hands and cover my eyes, shutting them tight. I'm afraid to open them. I expect to see Loving Leader's head pop out of the screen and jut into my face. I can just imagine him pointing his finger at me, blaming me for everything, calling me "different, dangerous, detrimental." And then skipping strike two entirely and sentencing me to the barren asteroid.

"Norbert," says Bucky Buckner.

I take a deep breath. I slowly open my eyes and peek between my fingers. I see a familiar face on the TruthScreen. But no, it's not Loving Leader! Far from it!

"Aunt Martha!" I take my hands from my face. "Is that you?" She sits on the dreary gray sofa in our dreary gray living room.

"Of course it's me," she replies. "Who were you expecting?"

"You didn't forget about me, did you?" asks Uncle Hank. He plops himself down on the sofa next to Aunt Martha.

"No, Uncle Hank, of course not! I miss you both a ton."

Bucky Buckner leaves his office and shuts the door. He lets me talk with my aunt and uncle—alone.

"We received your message," says Aunt Martha. "But we don't have the slightest idea what it means."

Dominic's divergent gibberish transducer changed my entire voice message into gobbledygook. For starters, the gizmo converted "Hello, Aunt Martha and Uncle Hank" into "Bongo, plant karma hand wrinkle spank." It translated my name to "North hurt biddle." And "when you get this message, please come get me" became "vcocoo jet miss wreckage, cheese thumb wet tree."

"We just want to make sure you're okay," says Uncle Hank. "When we received this odd message, we got so worried."

Aunt Martha nods. "We thought you'd lost your mind completely."

"No, I haven't lost my mind, but I'm going to lose it if you don't come get me right away." I beg them to rescue me. "Everyone else here is stark raving mad. They're all completely bananas."

Uncle Hank shakes his head. "You should have thought of that before you—"

"I'm sorry for everything I did. I'll never ever use my imagination again. Wait! What am I saying? I don't even have an imagination! Aunt Martha, Uncle Hank, please! I promise to conform. To blend in. To be like everyone else Just get me out of here! If you love me, if you care about me at all, get on the next spaceship and bring me back home!"

Aunt Martha and Uncle Hank turn to each other.

I see tears running down Aunt Martha's cheeks. Uncle Hank hands her his gray handkerchief.

"Honey, we can't," says Aunt Martha. She dries her eyes.

"We want to bring you back home," says Uncle Hank. "We really do."

"But you belong where you are," says Aunt Martha. "They can help you there. You're different, dear."

"And different is dangerous," says Uncle Hank. "Imagination is insanity. Creativity is crazy. Everyone knows that."

Now I'm crying too.

Aunt Martha places her hand on the TruthScreen as if reaching out to touch me. "I'm so sorry, Norbert. Really, I am."

I put my hand to the screen to touch her hand.

"Loving Leader sees all, knows all, and loves all," says Uncle Hank.

Now I get it. Aunt Martha and Uncle Hank think Loving Leader is eavesdropping on this very conversation. They're convinced the Truth Police know every little thing we're saying. They're too scared to help me. Too intimidated to tell me how they really feel. One wrong move, and what happened to my parents will happen to them.

"Please come get me!" I shout. "Please bring me home!"

The TruthScreen goes black. Aunt Martha and Uncle Hank are gone.

Now I'm crying like a baby.

Bucky knocks on the door and opens it a crack. "Okay if I come in?"

I wipe my eyes with the sleeve of my jumpsuit.

Bucky enters his office and leans against his desk. "So, Norbert, I'm afraid that's strike two."

I sink deeper into the chair. I feel like the cushions are going to swallow me whole. "What for?" I ask. "I didn't refuse to participate again." Well, that's not totally true. Drew, Sophie, and I did sneak out early from the Love Fest. But we definitely participated. Did Bucky see us leave?

Bucky taps his fingers on his desk. "You attempted to escape from Zorquat Three."

"I never tried to escape—"

"You sent a message to your aunt and uncle, telling them to steal a spaceship and come rescue you. What do you call that?"

"A practical joke?"

"Sorry, Norbert, attempting to escape is the ultimate refusal to participate. And I hear you did something else interesting last night."

Uh-oh. He knows about the watchtower.

The jig is up.

Chapter 24

scratch my head. "Last night? Hmmm. I don't remember doing anything interesting last night."

Bucky folds his arms across his chest. "I understand you did an impression of Loving Leader for everyone in your cabin."

The good news? Bucky has no idea we broke into the watchtower. *Phew!* Close call! The bad news? He knows all about the little show I performed from atop Crazy Swayzee's footlocker.

"Oh, that was nothing," I say.

"You made a mockery of Loving Leader."

"Me? No, I'd never poke fun at Loving Leader.

Honest. It was a loving tribute to His All-Knowing Eternal Excellency. I was telling everyone about the joy of conformity. How we should all conform and sacrifice our individuality for the greater good."

"Nice try, Norbert. That's a very creative answer."

"But I'm not trying to be creative. I don't want to be creative. Creativity is crazy. And I'm not crazy. I'm as dull as dishwater. Really, I am." Although I have to admit, back home dishwater is pretty exciting stuff. It's probably the most exciting thing in our house, if you want to know the truth. "I miss home. I miss my family. Send me back to Earth, Bucky. Please, I don't belong here."

Bucky places his hand on my shoulder. "Norbert, I know exactly where you belong. Come with me." He beckons me with his index finger.

I wince. I don't want to go anywhere. Except back home to Earth.

I clench the arms of the comfy chair. Tightly. I'd rather stay right here. In this chair. For the rest of my life. It's a pretty comfortable chair. Much more comfortable than that Black Box. That's for sure.

Bucky squints at me. He's getting ready to pinch

my ear and tug me up from the chair. That's the last thing I want. Well, the second-to-last thing. The last thing I want is to end up in the Black Box surrounded by creepy aliens.

I pick myself up from the chair and trail after him.

Bucky escorts me from his office. We tromp down the steps and then march across Astro-Nuts Camp. We pass the mess hall. The flagpole. The watchtower. My heart skips a beat.

As we cross the meadow, I feel other kids gawking at me, pointing, and whispering to one another. What are they saying? Do they know where Bucky is taking me? Do they know something I don't?

Their stares strike more fear into my heart. My anxiety rises to a fever pitch. I'm a bundle of nerves.

I consider running away. I can just make an abrupt U-turn, sprint into the woods, and hide among the trees. When night falls, I'll head for the hills. But where exactly would I go? What would I eat? What if I run into a gigantic extraterrestrial beast that picks me up like a mouse and swallows me in one quick gulp? And if I try to run away right now and Bucky catches me, will that just make things worse?

We walk toward the ominous Black Box. I hear screams. Yes, shrieks and yelps. From kids inside the box. There's definitely a group of kids trapped inside that thing. With scuzzy alien beings that ooze green slime from their fingertips.

Or giant blue spiders that trap you in their web, wrap you in their sticky silk, and eat you later as a midnight snack.

Or a humongous, gooey blob that engulfs and absorbs any other life-form it touches.

Now I'm scared to death. I'm ready to burst into tears again, but I hold them back. I don't want Bucky to see how frightened I am. I don't want to give him any power over me. None whatsoever.

Thankfully, Bucky escorts me past the dreaded Black Box. I catch my breath. My heart settles down. I can think clearly again.

I decide against making a run for it. I realize that would be a dumb move. Why risk getting a third strike and being sent to a barren asteroid now? I may as well just stick with Bucky and see what happens.

But where is Bucky taking me? Where do I belong?

Chapter 25

"Let's play badminton!" shouts Kitty Carpenter, Sophie's counselor.

We're standing in a large rotunda—a round room with a high domed ceiling.

A group of kids stand in a circle in the center of the chamber. They respond in enthusiastic unison. "Yes, let's play badminton!"

Without saying another word, they all start pretending—individually and silently—to play badminton. Some kids swing an imaginary racket at an imaginary birdie. hitting it back and forth over an imaginary net. Others kids pretend to miss the imaginary birdie and go looking for it in a corner of the room.

Suddenly Kitty Carpenter blows a whistle on a lanyard hanging around her neck. Everyone freezes in place.

"Okeydokey," Kitty calls out. "Let's go fishing!"

"Yes, let's go fishing!" reply the kids with gusto.

Then each kid starts pretend-fishing. Some kids put an imaginary worm on the end of an imaginary hook. They cast their imaginary fishing lines from an imaginary wharf. Others sit in imaginary rowboats. A girl named Keisha wades through an imaginary stream, swishing an imaginary net.

Kitty blows her whistle again. Everyone stops fishing. I'm guessing Kitty thinks they've caught enough fish for one day. I mean, how many imaginary fish do they really need? I wish they'd throw all the fish they caught back in the water. Otherwise, they're being cruel to those fish. Anyone can see that.

When Kitty blows her whistle, Bucky turns to me. "What do you think?"

"This is madness," I say.

"No, this is freedom," says Bucky. "The freedom to use your imagination."

"Imagination is insanity."

"No, Norbert. Imagination is freedom."

"But this is crazy."

"No, this is pantomime," explains Bucky.

"No, these pants are mine. Those pants are yours."

"You know, you're a funny kid."

"Funny ha-ha? Or funny strange?"

"Funny looking."

We both laugh.

Bucky explains that pantomime is acting without speaking any words—kind of like charades. "You try to get across the idea by using only gestures, movements, and facial expressions."

"Interesting," I admit. "But this really isn't my cup of tea. In fact, I don't even drink tea. Not even iced tea. Lemonade, sure. Tea? Definitely not."

"Are you refusing to participate?"

I tremble. "No, I'll play invisible badminton if you tell me to. I just think it's stupid."

"Okay, let's try something different."

"How many times do I have to tell you? I'm not different. Different is dangerous."

"No, Norbert, different is your destiny."

Chapter 26

With Bucky glued to me as my guide, we leave the rotunda and walk down a narrow hallway to a small auditorium. I really don't want a babysitter. I want my parents.

Onstage, that big shot Roger Payne stands alongside Charlene Gordon.

Other kids sit in the audience. They pay close attention.

The head girls' counselor, Large Marge, stands onstage—off to the side. She wears a black-and-white-striped referee's shirt. "We're playing Yay!/Boo!" she announces. "The topic is gruel." As soon as

Bucky and I take our seats in the audience, Large Marge straightens the horned Viking helmet on her head, raises a whistle to her lips, and blows. The game commences.

Charlene says something positive. "I love gruel! It's my favorite food! I eat gruel every day for breakfast, lunch, and dinner!"

The kids in the audience yell, "Yay!"

Roger must respond with a negative statement. "And now you weigh five hundred pounds from eating all that gruel."

The kids in the audience yell, "Boo!"

Charlene and Roger must continue going back and forth, making positive and negative statements to advance their story—until one of them fumbles, can't think of anything to say, or replies with something completely off topic.

"Sure, I've gained a ton of weight, but that gives me a great reason to exercise to get back in shape," says Charlene. *Yay!*

"Too bad Loving Leader outlawed all exercise! Except for filing paperwork!" *Boo!*

Charlene smacks her own face in astonishment.

"I love filing paperwork! In fact, I love filing paperwork while I eat gruel!" *Yay!*

Roger wags his finger. "But now all your paperwork is covered with gruel and the pages stick together." *Boo!*

"Yes, gruel doubles as glue! It's the strongest glue in the world! You can also use gruel just like concrete to build homes, factories, roads, and bridges." *Yay!*

Roger scowls. "But when the rain comes, all those houses and factories melt into gruel again. And then gruel floods the streets and people get stuck in the gruel, which swallows them alive." *Boo!*

I'm laughing hysterically. I can't believe how fast and funny Charlene and Roger are. It's like watching an imaginary badminton birdie bounce back and forth over an imaginary net. I'm awed by their wit.

Charlene pokes her finger in the air. "My friends and I hold gruel-eating contents to see who can eat the most gruel!" *Yay!*

Roger is clearly stumped. Large Marge nearly blows her whistle.

But Roger bounces back just in the nick of time. "And they all get sick to their stomach and end up vomiting gruel." *Boo!*

Charlene giggles. "Not me! That's why I always win! And now I'm the gruel-eating champion of the world!" *Yay!*

Large Marge blows her whistle, ending the game. It's a tie.

Everyone in the audience applauds and cheers. Roger may be a show-off, but I have to admit, he's really clever and quick witted. And Charlene...I mean, wow! What an imagination!

Whoops! Did I just say that out loud?

I look around the room. Sergeant Sergeant sits alone in the back of the theater, observing everything, a sinister smile on his face. Creepy, really.

Is he watching me?

I get the feeling there's something funny going on. And not just onstage.

Chapter 27

Seeing Sergeant Sergeant in the back row makes me more nervous than a chicken at a fox convention. Is he looking for a reason to convince Bucky to give me strike three?

I look to Bucky. "What's this all about?" I ask.

Bucky puts on his dark sunglasses. I'm not sure exactly why. After all, we're still inside the auditorium. "Improv," he says.

"What's improv?"

"It's short for 'improvisation.'"

"Great. That explains nothing."

"Improv is a type of acting, but the actors make

up everything right on the spot. Without any preparation whatsoever. It's completely spontaneous. Just like you saw Roger and Charlene do just now."

"How do they do that?"

Bucky waves to Charlene and signals her to join us. "Why don't you ask Charlene?"

I don't know what to say. I'm completely tonguetied. I squirm in my seat. Finally I manage to blurt out a few garbled sounds. "Uh, sure."

Charlene perches herself on the edge of the stage, her legs dangling over the side. She folds her hands on her lap. Her blond hair cascades over her shoulders. I'm in heaven. It's a nice break from exile on Zorquat 3.

Bucky removes his sunglasses. "Charlene, I'd like you to meet one of our new Astro-Nuts." Silence. He nudges me with his elbow. "That's your cue to introduce yourself."

"Oh." I've completely forgotten my name. I look into Charlene's eyes. They're deep blue pools and I long to tread water. "My name. Right. I'm sorry...."

"Nice to meet you, Sorry. That's a very interesting name." She giggles.

"Thank you. My friends call me Norbert. My real name is Norbert Riddle. The Truth Police affectionately call me Nonperson Number L4LUZR-1. They're very caring."

SOMEONE JUST STOLE MY HEART.

Bucky clears his throat. "Norbert has a question for you."

"I do?" My mind has suddenly gone blank. "Oh yes, I do. I was wondering how you learned to do that."

"Do what?"

"Improv. That's the name for it, right? You're really funny."

Charlene smiles. "Thank you. That's really nice of you to say. We practice. A lot. We play different improv games to sharpen our comedy skills. It's like anything. The more you practice, the better you get."

"Yeah, just like imaginary badminton." I hold my imaginary racket and serve an imaginary birdie. I pop my lips to mimic the sound.

She laughs. "You should give improv a try."

"Me? I wouldn't know where to start."

"We take a suggestion from the audience to get you started. It's really not as hard as it looks." She tosses me that beautiful smile and takes my hand in hers. "C'mon, Sorry, don't be shy."

My heart goes pitter-patter.

Charlene hops down and brings me to the referee standing at the foot of the stage. "Marge, could this new kid please give Yay!/Boo! a whirl? This is Sorry. I mean, Norbert."

Large Marge looks to Bucky Buckner. The warden nods, and strokes his mustache.

Charlene gives my hand a squeeze for luck and then sends me up the steps to the stage. I stand alongside Roger Payne. Out in the audience, Sergeant Sergeant glares at me from the back of the room.

Roger straightens his posture, tugs the lapels of his corduroy blazer, and fluffs up his ascot. Holding his head high, he peers down his nose at me, crosses his eyes, and sticks out his tongue. I guess that's his trademark move.

Large Marge addresses us both. "Now remember, every improv performance is unique. It's different every time. Relax, just respond naturally to everything that's said. This is how we learn to interact with each other onstage—without planning a thing."

We play rock-paper-scissors to decide who goes first. I throw out a rock, and Roger throws out scissors, so I win the serve.

When Large Marge blows her whistle, I have to start the game with a positive statement worthy of a "Yay!"

Roger looks ready to rumble. Me? I'm ready to crumble.

"Good luck, New Kid," says Roger. "You're going to need it."

Thanks for the support, Mr. Warmth.

Large Marge turns to the audience. "All right, I need a topic."

"Backward Day," shouts one kid.

"Spaghetti and meatballs," yells another.

"The Truth Police," comes a suggestion from the back of the room.

I look out into the audience. Sergeant Sergeant leans back in his seat, with his feet up on the seat back in front of him, and smirks at me.

"All right, the topic is..." Large Marge places the whistle between her lips. "The Truth Police."

She blows her whistle.

Game on.

Chapter 28

can't believe I'm standing on an actual stage in front of an audience. Everyone's staring at me. Of course, that's what audiences do. I guess I should have expected that.

I'm having a little trouble coming up with something positive to say about the Truth Police. Realizing this is my chance to convince Bucky I'm Mr. Conformity, I bust out with: "The Truth Police are the kindest and most caring people in the world."

The kids in the audience give me a lukewarm

"Yay!" They're not big fans of the Truth Police. I can't imagine why—probably because I have no imagination.

Roger spikes up his hair with his hand. "But the Truth Police are mean to anyone who's creative, imaginative, or innovative," he says.

The audience roars a collective "Boo!"

"The Truth Police would be nicer to everyone if they got treated with more respect!" *Yay!*

Sergeant Sergeant nods. He taps the screen of this Truthcorder. Is he taking notes?

Roger leans over to get in my face. "They don't deserve any respect! They're cruel puppets working for an oppressive tyrant." *Boo!*

"That's why we have to start holding special Love Fests to demonstrate our love for the Truth Police! We'll show Loving Leader how deeply we love the Truth Police!" *Yay!*

"Then the Truth Police will arrest us for protesting!" *Boo!*

"But love conquers all, and if we all shower the Truth Police with our unconditional love, the Truth

Police will shower us right back with their love in return." *Yay!*

"They'll shower us, all right, you dumb clown. They'll shower us with tear gas and pepper spray." *Boo!*

"Well, that's great, Roger, because you really need a shower!" *Yay!*

Everyone in the room cheers like crazy. Apparently, most of them feel the same way about Roger Payne as I do.

Roger doesn't know what to say next. He's speechless. Totally stumped. Startled that I just took him down a notch.

Large Marge blows her whistle. She races over and raises my arm in the air. I'm declared the winner of my first improv game. Unbelievable. I'm more stunned than Roger is.

Bucky Buckner rises from his seat in the front row a gives me a high five. "Well played, Norbert. Way to go!"

I hop down from the stage.

"You're really funny," says Charlene. She gives me a hug. "I'm really proud of you. That took a lot of courage."

Okay, I admit it. That was fun. I'm eating up the attention. Maybe I do belong here. Maybe I'm more imaginative than I realize.

My eyes dart around the theater. Sitting in the back of the audience, Sergeant Sergeant shoots me a dirty look and sneers. I guess he's mad I didn't slip into his trap and make Bucky give me one last strike.

Large Marge pats me on the back. "You're a natural, Norbert. We'd love to have you join our improv group. Consider this a formal invitation. What do you say? It's a lot of fun."

Her kind offer catches me completely off guard. "I...uh...I'm not sure."

Bucky raises his eyebrows. He grabs hold of an imaginary baseball bat and pretends to take a swing in the air. Like I really need someone reminding me how many strikes I have.

The problem is, I don't want anyone thinking I'm different and dangerous. Not Bucky Buckner. Not Large Marge. And certainly not Sergeant Sergeant.

Besides, I honestly don't know if I'm clever enough to keep up with everyone else. It's a little intimidating. And by "a little," I mean tremendously.

Although, I wouldn't mind spending more time with Charlene Gordon. She's smart, funny, and super nice. Adorable, too. I'd really like to learn more about her. Like why she eats only with chopsticks.

Charlene caresses my hand. "Say yes, Norbert." She gazes into my eyes.

"Yes, Norbert." I'm totally smitten. I guess you could say I've gone completely gaga.

Smiling, Bucky leaves the auditorium.

Sergeant Sergeant still leers at me. He frantically taps the screen of his Truthcorder.

"You won't be sorry," says Large Marge. "You've definitely got the spark."

"The spark?"

"The spark of imagination," says Charlene.

I hold a finger to my lips. "Shhh! Not so loud!"

My eyes scour the room to check whether Sergeant Sergeant overheard any of this conversation.

Sergeant Sergeant and his Truthcorder are no longer in the audience.

Did I luck out after all?

few days go by. Three, to be precise.

But remember, I'm talking about three days on Zorquat 3. Not Earth.

Like I said before, eight days here equal seven days on Earth.

To make the Astro-Nuts calendar jibe with the Earth calendar, Bucky Buckner added one more day to the week here on Zorquat 3. Pretty simple, really. Unless you find this confusing.

On the Astro-Nuts calendar, sandwiched between Sunday and Monday, is the eighth day of the week. It's called Someday. As in "Someday my prince will come." Or "I'll get around to it Someday." Or "Someday I'll be old enough to stay up past midnight."

I know it sounds crazy. That's because Somedays definitely are crazy — with a capital Z.

I'm bringing all this up because today is Someday. And on Someday everyone at Astro-Nuts Camp gets a full day of free time. We can do anything we want, anything at all. Well, almost anything. I can't take a spaceship back to Earth or find out where my parents are. Maybe Someday soon.

Today Charlene Gordon invites me, Drew, and Sophie to go swimming with her and her friends Keisha, Jasmine, and Zach.

We hike to the waterfall that cascades from the top of the tall mountain that towers high above the others. The waterfall spills into a beautiful lake surrounded by tall trees. The bright yellow ball shines high in the sky.

Charlene and I sit together on a flat boulder on the shore, while Drew and Sophie splash together in the water. Keisha, Jasmine, and Zach walk around the lake to explore the waterfall and get sprayed with mist.

I can't believe I'm alone with my dream girl. My heart is racing at super-duper-hyper-turbo-zippo-speed. I'm too nervous to speak. Of course, I'm not exactly sure what to say in the first place.

"So, Norbert, why were you so afraid to join my improv group?"

I look deep into her eyes. Someone once said, "The eyes are the windows to your soul." For me, that's exactly what I see looking into Charlene's eyes. Her beautiful soul. When she gazes into my eyes, I know she sees who I really am too.

"It's like you're scared to be your true self," she says.

"No, I'm not."

"Norbert, you're wearing a gray jumpsuit at the beach."

"It's my favorite color."

"C'mon, what gives?"

I refuse to answer unless Charlene tells me why she eats only with chopsticks.

"That's top secret classified information," she says.

"So's mine."

"Okay, I'll spill the beans," says Charlene. "But you go first."

She holds my hand and waits patiently. She knows this will be tough for me.

It's like we've always known each other, which is strange, because we met only a few days ago. I know it sounds crazy, but I feel like I can tell Charlene anything.

"I was five years old when my parents disappeared." I stop there. I almost never get much further than that.

Charlene caresses my shoulder. "It's okay. Take your time."

"It was night. The three of us were sitting on the sofa together in our house, watching the TruthScreen. Suddenly, from out of nowhere, the Truth Police burst into our house. My mother screamed. 'What do you think you're doing?' my father demanded. 'Get out of this house this instant!'

"But they didn't listen. My mother yelled, 'Show me your warrant! Show me your warrant!' Over and over again. I still hear her voice echoing in my head. 'Show me your warrant!'

"'We don't need no stinkin' warrant,' said the Truth Police. 'Ezra Riddle! You're under arrest for being different and dangerous.'

"To this day, those two words send chills up my spine. Different and dangerous. My father wasn't different and dangerous. He was the inventor of the TruthScreen. But the Truth Police didn't care about that. They handcuffed his wrists behind his back and took him away to be 'reeducated.'"

I picture it all over again, clear as day. Even though it happened at night.

My eyes start to mist. Just like the waterfall off in the distance.

Charlene's eyes start welling up too. "I don't understand. Why would the Truth Police arrest your father?"

Good question.

Chapter 30

harlene wraps her arm around my shoulders. Her warm embrace gives me the courage to share the rest of my story.

"Well, this may sound hard to believe," I say, "but the TruthScreen was never supposed to be used by the government to spy on people. My father did not invent the TruthScreen for surveillance purposes.

"He created the TruthScreen so people could make video calls from one TruthScreen to another TruthScreen. Watch television shows, movies, and sporting events. Share photos and videos. Do homework together, participate in game shows, improve communication. He called his invention the Truth-Screen because he wanted to spread the truth. Not fear. He wanted to make the world a better place. Not worse.

"Everyone wanted a TruthScreen. It was the coolest invention ever, and everyone bought one. People hung a TruthScreen in every room of the house, every office, every restaurant, every classroom. Until there were TruthScreens everywhere.

"But when Loving Leader seized control of the government, he also seized control of the Truth-Screen. And, well, you know the rest."

"What happened to your mother?" asks Charlene. "I thought the Truth Police arrested her, too."

"They did, but not right away. At first they didn't consider her different and dangerous." My whole body shivers. "The Truth Police left my mother to take care of me. She was an avant-garde artist. Maybe you've heard of her…Yoshiko Riddle."

Charlene shakes her head no. "Tell me about her."

"Well, right after my father disappeared, my mother began painting a bunch of pictures of the Truth Police arresting my father. A famous art gallery agreed to exhibit the paintings. But right before opening night, the Truth Police burst into our house and declared my mother…"

"Different and dangerous."

I'm trying hard not to get all choked up. "They arrested her, sent her away to be 'reeducated,' and confiscated all of her paintings. I never saw my mother or father again. I have no idea where they are."

I stop for a moment to catch my breath. I hear strange sounds. The rustle of leaves. Footsteps in the woods. The clinking of military medals. Startled, I glimpse the nearby bushes and shrubs.

Sergeant Sergeant stands, poorly hidden, amidst the green foliage with a Truthcorder in his grip, as usual. He's spying on us. No doubt about it. He's trying to catch me doing something wrong so he can report me to Bucky and get me strike three. I just know it.

When he notices me looking straight at him, he turns his attention to his Truthcorder and taps the screen a few times, as if he's just categorizing plants and butterflies. I decide to ignore him. After all, I'm not doing anything wrong.

I turn back to Charlene. "I don't want to end up lost forever like my parents. I don't want to be different and dangerous. I don't need to be creative or express my individuality. I just want to return home, find my mother and father, and live happily ever after."

"In a bleak gray world run by Loving Leader."

I shrug. "If that's what it takes to be with my parents."

"Then why did you do what you did to get here?" asks Charlene.

Tears well up in my eyes. "Because my teacher, Mrs. Hurlbutt, went to the bathroom."

Charlene looks at me like I'm crazy. "I don't understand."

"She told us to be on our best behavior while she was gone, 'so no one gets arrested by the Truth Police and mysteriously disappears, never to be heard from again. *Like Norbert's parents!*'"

Teardrops trickle down my face.

Charlene gasps. "That's horrible. What a nasty old biddy."

"I lost control. All my pent-up hatred for Loving

Leader came rushing out of me. I jumped on top of Mrs. Hurlbutt's desk and did a wild impression of Loving Leader."

Charlene gives me a huge, affectionate hug. She holds me for a long time. I feel safe.

For a brief moment I don't care if I ever see that dreary gray house again.

"Okay, Charlene, your turn. Why do you eat only with chopsticks?"

I hear more stomping in the trees, much louder than before. I turn to look, expecting to find Sergeant Sergeant invading my personal space.

Instead I'm confronted by the terrifying face of...

A vicious brontosaurus.

Chapter 31

Being the clever kid that I am, I take immediate action. I scream.

The brontosaurus screams too, revealing its sharp, pointy teeth and billowing a cloud of its nasty breath right in my face.

Ugh! Its breath smells worse than Mrs. Hurlbutt's perfume, Butt Thunder. That's not the perfume's real name. That's just what I call it. I bet Butt Thunder would be a huge hit among skunks.

The brontosaurus and I are both seeing eye to eye, which doesn't make either one of us very happy. The brontosaurus snarls. I do the same.

"Don't you worry none," I hear a familiar voice say from high above.

I look up into the bright yellow ball in the sky. I place my hand over my eyebrows to improvise a visor. I'm the king of low-budget fashion. Just ask Farley Chung.

Swayzee is sitting in a saddle on the back of the brontosaurus. He's wearing a cowboy hat and tall snakeskin boots. Swayzee, not the brontosaurus.

"She's docile. Ain't that right, girl?" Crazy Swayzee pets the brontosaurus at the base of her long neck, which is purple with large pink spots, sort of like a giraffe. Quite unusual. Then again, so is a living brontosaurus.

The brontosaurus nods and makes a curious purring sound.

"Docile? What's that supposed to mean?" I'm nervous that the word "docile" is another way of saying "hungry," "famished," or "convinced you'd taste pretty good—even without ketchup or mustard."

"I don't have the foggiest idea," says Swayzee. "But 'docile' sure sounds friendly, don't it? Why don't you and your friends hop aboard? We're all headed out to the forest to test Dominic's latest invention."

Behind Swayzee's brontosaurus, a bunch of my cabin mates from unit 16 ride on the backs of other brontosauruses with entirely different patterns. Roger Payne sits atop a striped brontosaurus, Farley Chung rides an argyle one, and Howie Rubenstein snaps away with his camera from atop a paisley brontosaurus.

I turn to Charlene. "What do you think?"

"Sounds intriguing," says Charlene. She takes me by the hand.

"Well, me oh my," says Swayzee. "What do we have here?"

"Yeah, what do we have here?" comes a voice from behind me.

I swing around.

Sophie stands with her hands on her hips and a big frown on her face.

"Sophie, don't be silly. You already know Charlene."

"Do I?" asks Sophie. "I'm not sure I really do."

"Hey, what's going on between you two?" Drew dries himself with a towel.

"That's what I'd like to know," says Sophie.

Something's bugging Sophie. I'm not sure what. Guessing she feels left out, I extend the invitation. "Swayzee invited us all out to the forest to test Dominic's latest invention. You guys wanna go?"

"What are these things?" Drew points to the herd of brontosauruses.

"Gonzosauruses," says Swayzee. "Unique to this planet."

That takes me by surprise. "I thought they were brontosauruses."

"Nope, brontosauruses lived only on Earth, until they went extinct."

"Really? When did they go extinct? Nobody tells me anything." Of course I'm just being a wise guy.

Swayzee gives me the side eye. "Brontosauruses and gonzosauruses sure do look alike," he says. "But the brontosaurus had a brain the size of a golf ball. A gonzosaurus's brain is the size of a grapefruit."

I turn to Charlene. "Why do we always compare the size of things to a golf ball or a grapefruit? From now on I'm comparing the size of hail to a gonzosaurus's brain."

"And gonzosauruses are much more fashionable," says Farley Chung.

"Too bad smelly breath hasn't gone out of style," I add.

Sophie raises her hand to ask a question. Not that she needs to. "What did Dominic invent?"

Swayzee straightens the cowboy hat on his head. "There's only one way to find out."

Chapter 32

Swayzee's gonzosaurus lowers her tail and—in one fell swoop—scoops up both Charlene and me. We slide down her strong tail to join Swayzee on her back.

"Well, well," says Swayzee. "It looks like Norbert Riddle has good taste after all."

"Why, thank you," says Charlene. She wraps her arms around Swayzee's waist.

"This here's Princess."

The gonzosaurus smiles at me, nods, and...winks.

"I think Princess likes you," says Swayzee.

"That's terrific." I wrap my arms around

Charlene's waist. "As long as she doesn't like me for dinner."

"I reckon we'll just have to see about that. She obviously heard about your good taste."

The striped gonzosaurus reaches down with its tail, scoops up Sophie, and places her behind Roger Payne. The argyle gonzosaurus does the same thing with Drew, plopping him behind Farley Chung.

From the saddle of his paisley gonzosaurus, Howie snaps artsy photos of the proceedings. He's as happy as my aunt Martha when Uncle Hank takes out the trash.

Keisha, Jasmine, and Zach prefer to stay behind at the waterfall. They're content splashing about and frolicking in the mist.

"Giddyup!" shouts Swayzee.

The gonzosauruses lift their heads and start traipsing along the river and into the forest.

"Do you know how to steer one of these things?" asks Drew.

Farley straightens the argyle handkerchief in the breast pocket of his jacket. I notice it matches the argyle of his gonzosaurus. "Honestly? No."

"You sure know how to inspire confidence."

"This big guy drives himself. Say hello to Boomer."

Boomer joggles his head and purrs.

The river slowly narrows until the gonzosauruses are slogging through mud knee-deep.

Sophie tightens her grip around Roger Payne's waist. "So really, what's going on with those two?" she asks Roger, nodding toward me and Charlene.

"Just something we stage actors call chemistry."

I turn around and give Sophie the eye. "You know, both Charlene and I have excellent hearing."

Roger chuckles. "What's your passion, Sophie?"

"I love making music."

"I bet we could make beautiful music together."

Sophie rolls her eyes. "Well, you're definitely starting out on the wrong note. What's *your* passion?"

Roger raises his hand in the air for dramatic effect. "Acting."

"Then you should really try acting nice," says Sophie.

Roger grins. "To tell you the truth, I think you're one in a million."

"That's sweet, but honestly, so are your chances."

"C'mon, Sophie, where's your heart?"

"Straight down my throat, first turn to the left."

I'm cracking up. Roger and Sophie have no idea how funny they are together. "You two definitely have a unique chemistry."

Charlene laughs. "I think Roger's only interested in biology."

The gonzosauruses carry us through a swampy marsh. Thick vines droop from tree branches overhead. Flowers with oblong petals sweeten the air.

We tromp through the forest and reach a lush valley. In the clearing sits a tumbledown shed and several rickety workbenches.

Princess lowers her head to the ground, and Swayzee slides down her long neck, followed by me and Charlene. All the other kids slide down the necks of their gonzosauruses to join us on the ground.

Dominic and a group of his techie pals reveal their invention. They've built a bunch of helicycles — pedal-powered helicopters! The bizarre contraptions are parked all over the field.

I examine one of the machines. It's basically a unicycle with handlebars and lightweight helicopter blades. "How do you fly this thing?" I ask.

"Just take a seat and crank the pedals," says Dominic. "A thin rubber belt looped around the tire rim spins the helicopter rotor, turning the blades, which lift this sucker high into the sky," he explains. "Go ahead, Norbert. Take it for a spin."

Me? Is he crazy?

Chapter 33

'm pretty convinced these pedal-powered helicopters will never get off the ground. "There's just no way anyone can possibly pedal fast enough to lift off from the earth."

"That's the beauty of all this," says Dominic. "We're not on Earth. There's twenty-five percent less gravity here on Zorquat Three. That works to our advantage, aerodynamically speaking."

Dominic makes an excellent point. I think. Honestly, I don't know the first thing about aerodynamics. But I do know the second thing about aerodynamics—a human-powered helicopter could easily crash.

That's why I don't want to be Dominic's guinea pig. And also because I know for a fact that guinea pigs did not originate in Guinea, West Africa. They're from South America. And they're not really pigs at all. They're rodents. And I definitely don't want to be a rat. One Sergeant Sergeant is plenty.

"Okay, who wants to test-fly a helicycle?" asks Dominic.

None of the other kids volunteer. Neither does Crazy Swayzee.

Drew smiles and steps forward. "I'll give it whirl," he says.

"This ought to be good," says Roger.

Sophie shushes him and steps over to Drew's side. "I admire your courage," she says.

Drew puts on a plastic helmet and buckles the strap. "Courage doesn't mean I'm not scared to death. I'm just not afraid to do what I'm afraid to do—if you know what I mean."

Sophie gives Drew a bear hug. "Good luck," she says. "I know you can do it."

"If anything happens to me, I just want you to know…" Drew stops.

Sophie stares at him. "Know what?"

"Having a warm heart in a cold world takes courage too."

She kisses him on the cheek.

Dominic holds the helicycle steady as Drew hops aboard the seat and grips the handlebars.

"Ready?" asks Dominic.

"No. But that's never stopped me before."

Drew starts pedaling. The chopper blades begin spinning faster and faster. They whoosh through the air.

Howie snaps pictures like crazy.

Why do I get the feeling this could all go horribly wrong?

The helicycle trembles and shakes. It looks ready to topple over. But with a sudden jolt, the kooky contraption levitates up an inch. It abruptly drops to the ground, bumps back upward, and then rises into the air.

Within seconds Drew hovers high above us, suspended in the sky. "Wow! This is awesome!" he shouts.

The rest of us immediately race to grab one of the many helicycles scattered about the field. We strap on helmets, hop aboard, and start pedaling like mad, keen on letting our spirits soar.

One by one, we each rise high in the sky, floating alongside Drew. We must be a zillion miles above the ground. Or at least one.

"Holy moly, look at that!" Charlene points to the panoramic view of Astro-Nuts Camp far below us in the distance.

From this height everything looks so small. Tiny cabins and bungalows surround a little green meadow. When I squint, I can barely make out the flower boxes lining the bottom of each window. In the middle of the meadow, an itsy-bitsy red flag waves atop a wooden flagpole the size of a toothpick.

I see the amphitheater, where the Love Fest took place. I point to the mess hall and the Black Box. I spot the watchtower sticking out from the treetops. I wonder if Sergeant Sergeant is peering through his high-powered binoculars right now, watching us fly between the two moons.

"Hey, everyone follow me!" exclaims Crazy Swayzee.

We learn quickly that turning the handlebars controls a rudder, allowing us to fly our helicycles wherever we wish to go.

We fly over the mountaintop that rises high above the others. The waterfall roars as it spills from a crag in the peak. I picture Keisha, Jasmine, and Zach beneath the cloud of mist, still swimming under the waterfall. From this altitude we can all see what lies beyond Astro-Nuts Camp.

There's a large desert. And by "large," I mean ginormous. I'm talking massive sand dunes that seem to stretch forever.

Far off in the distance, beyond the vast desert, sit hundreds of huge eggs. Some piled together, others scattered around. The eggs are all different colors, each with a completely different pattern. Stripes, polka dots, argyle, paisley, arabesque, latticework. You name it.

"What are those?" I ask.

"Gonzosaurus eggs," says Drew. "But you can't reach those nests without crossing Danger Desert. And Danger Desert isn't your typical desert. That sand you see is high-speed quicksand. It sucks you in ten times faster than regular quicksand. And you know what lives beneath it? Big, hairy creatures— sort of like giant octopuses—that reach up, wrap their huge tentacles around you, and pull you deep into the sand."

The thought of being devoured by a giant, hairy octopus flips me out, but then I realize Drew is just making stuff up again.

"Actually, it's much worse than that," says Swayzee.

My heart stops.

Well, not really. Just my legs stop. Pedaling, that is.

My helicycle plunges. I nearly lose my balance. My feet slip off the pedals.

"Whoooooooaaaaaaaa!"

Chapter 34

My helicycle spirals downward, whorling out of control. I'm falling out of the sky. Fast!

The good news? With 25 percent less gravity here on Zorquat 3, I'm falling at a speed 25 percent slower than I would be on Earth. *Yay!*

The bad news? I'm still plummeting to the ground. And that usually doesn't end well. *Boo!*

Fortunately, I won't have to clean up the mess. *Yay!*

I'm totally freaking out. And getting really dizzy from all the spinning. Out of the corner of my eye, I see someone swooping down on another helicycle.

It's Drew. He can't get close enough to rescue me without getting our blades tangled up—and causing both of us to crash.

Instead he keeps his distance and starts yelling something. I can't hear a word he's screaming. He rotates his clenched fists around each other, making a rapid pedaling motion.

Then it hits me. No, not the ground. What Drew is trying to tell me.

I straighten the handlebars, regaining my balance. My feet find the pedals and start spinning at lightning speed.

The thin blades overhead spin rapidly, and my descent slows. I hover for a few moments, suspended in air. Then the helicycle and I start rising back upward!

I slowly regain my composure, which is a good thing, because Dominic Garcia forgot to give us airsick bags.

Phew! Catastrophe averted. Talk about a close shave. Not bad considering I'm too young to shave.

With Drew by my side, I pedal like a maniac, lifting my helicycle to new heights. We're back alongside the others.

"Norbert, are you all right?" asks Sophie. "You really had me worried."

"Me too," says Charlene. "You scared me half to death."

I'm huffing and puffing. "I know just how you felt. Well, double that, actually."

Sophie flies up alongside Drew. "That was a really brave thing you just did. I'm so proud of you."

"Yes indeedy! Drew did a bang-up job," says Swayzee. "Without the bang-up, if you get my meaning."

Roger Payne pouts. "Anyone could have done it. Of course, I would have gone in with a lot more panache."

"Don't mind Roger none," says Swayzee. "He thinks the sun rises in the morning just to hear him crow."

Charlene swoops in alongside me. "I'm so glad you're okay. Listen, if you don't want to join my improv group, you can just say so. No need to do anything that drastic."

Dominic joins me. "Nice save, Norbert. I thought you were going to splat for sure."

"Splat? No way! Not with this cheap plastic helmet to protect me."

"Hey, who wants to see something cool?" asks Swayzee.

We all shrug. *Sure, why not?*

"Follow me over yonder." Swayzee turns his handlebars. The rudder steers his helicycle toward the tall mountaintop.

We trail behind Swayzee, flying over the roaring waterfall and toward the mountain peak. We gently land our helicycles on the summit and park them on the alpine grass.

Swayzee shows us the small treetop platform he built, from timber lashed together with rope, where one end of a thick wire is fastened. "This here's what you call a zip line. I tied the other end of the wire to the top of the flagpole way down yonder in the meadow. Ready to zip back down to Astro-Nuts Camp?"

Everyone cheers.

Dominic demonstrates how to fold up the helicopter blades on our helicycles. He turns his folded contraption upside down and places the grooved rim of the unicycle wheel on the cable. Standing on the wooden platform, he grabs firm hold of the handlebars.

"Sweet! Let's bounce! Three, two, one…" He sprints toward the end of the platform. "Cowabunga!" Dominic leaps off the mountain peak and disappears into a crag.

We hold our breath.

Suddenly he appears again. *"Waaaa-heeeeee!"* In a flash he zips down the cable to Astro-Nuts Camp.

Charlene turns her folded helicycle upside down and hangs the grooved rim of the unicycle wheel on the cable. She grips the handlebars and looks to me.

I scratch the back of my head. "I'm not so sure I want to risk my life again. I really just want to find out why you eat only with chopsticks."

"I'll tell you everything," she says. "As soon as we get to the flagpole."

Chapter 35

I decide to join Charlene's improv group, mostly just to spend time with Charlene. Well, that's not totally true. Don't tell anyone I said this, but I really enjoy the improv games. They're actually a lot of fun. But let's just keep that our little secret. I'm still pretending to be a conformist loyal to Loving Leader—to convince Bucky to send me home to Earth so I can find my parents.

I just figure if I'm stuck on this planet until Grissom returns with the spaceship, I may as well enjoy the good food, great friends, and fun activities. After all, life here on Zorquat 3 is pretty sweet. Besides, if I have to bide my time somewhere, I'd much rather play improv games with Charlene and the gang than break boulders on a barren asteroid for the rest of my life.

And I'm hoping the improv games will help me think up a foolproof way to snag Sergeant Sergeant's Truthcorder and get into my permanent record—without getting strike three.

I still refuse to wear anything but my gray jumpsuit. That's part of my master plan to convince Bucky I'm just a typical schlub.

Drew spends most of his time with a bunch of other artists and writers, creating an Astro-Nuts comic book. Every night he shows me his new drawings. So far he's drawn a whole bunch of cartoons of us riding gonzosauruses through the forest and pedaling helicycles high over the mountaintop.

Sophie has found her groove too. She plays keyboard and bells with a group of really talented musicians. She composes some awesome tunes and even writes the lyrics herself.

As for me, I'm sitting in a circle with Charlene, Roger, Keisha, Jasmine, and Zach. Large Marge is teaching us a bunch of cool improv games.

There's Expert Challenge, where you have to give a speech, pretending you're an expert on whatever the topic is. Like middle school, thumbtack inventory, or stuffing cotton into aspirin bottles.

I love the game Slide Show. Large Marge chooses the topic of my slide show, like "My Vacation to Zorquat 3." Charlene and Zach strike a random posture and position, and I describe the scene in the "slide." Then I use my imaginary remote control to flip to the next slide, and Charlene and Zach strike a new pose. I've made up some crazy descriptions.

Now Large Marge asks for a suggestion. "I need a tool or utensil," she says.

"A hammer," says Zach.

"A toothbrush," says Keisha.

"Chopsticks," says Charlene.

Large Marge straightens the Viking helmet on her head. "Okay, we're going to create the wackiest instruction manual for chopsticks that you can think up. Roger, give me the first direction."

Roger nods and begins. "Before using chopsticks, stand up and take a bow to properly set the stage for your performance. Sit down and take one chopstick in each hand. Say, 'Maestro, if you will...drumroll, please.' And then use the chopsticks to play a drum-roll on your table."

Large Marge points to me. "Norbert, please continue."

"Step two," I say. "Carefully place the chopsticks in the corners of your mouth, facing down. Presto! You're a walrus."

Large Marge points to Charlene. "Any warnings?"
"Never hold chopsticks like knitting needles.

Otherwise, you risk turning a plateful of noodles into a sweater," Charlene says.

Something outside one of the windows suddenly catches Roger's attention.

I follow his gaze. There's someone standing outside the window, peeking through the curtains. Someone in a uniform with medals on his chest. Yep, it's Sergeant Sergeant. He makes eye contact with Roger and winks.

Roger nods back.

I get the uneasy feeling there's something fishy going on.

Fortunately, Sergeant Sergeant takes off. Roger returns his attention to our group.

I breathe a sigh of relief. Maybe the whole thing was nothing.

Large Marge is now teaching us a new game, Mystery Date. She chooses Charlene to be the first player and sends her out of the room. She asks the rest of us to suggest names of real people.

"Bucky Buckner," says Keisha.

"Crazy Swayzee," says Zach.

"Loving Leader." Roger smirks. "Norbert does a fantastic impression of His All-Knowing Eternal Excellency. You really have to see it, Marge."

Just my luck.

Chapter 36

"Terrific," says Large Marge. "Norbert, you sit in this chair and pretend to be Loving Leader. Jasmine, you go get Charlene."

I'm not happy about this. Roger is up to something. I can just tell.

Charlene and Jasmine return to the room.

Large Marge tells Charlene to sit in a chair facing me. "All right, Charlene, behind this imaginary wall sits your mystery date. You have one minute to ask questions to guess who your mystery date is."

Charlene rubs her chin. "Mystery Date, where would you take me on our first date?"

That's easy. "To my surveillance room. So together we could watch everyone on the whole planet."

"How would you describe yourself?"

"I would call myself a fun-loving guy. No one else would ever call me that, but I would. I'm also very caring. So caring that I banish people I don't like to other planets...to protect the citizens of Earth from themselves!"

Roger snickers. He puts his hand over his mouth to contain his laughter.

Charlene smiles. "How would you feel about meeting my family on our first date?"

"I already know all about them. I've got my eye on them, believe you me. And if they don't abide by the rules, I'll definitely meet them again soon."

Howie Rubenstein steps into the room and starts snapping photos of Charlene and me in action.

Charlene crosses her legs. "What's your favorite song?"

"The Pledge of Subservience. It's actually not a song, but I love hearing citizens recite in unison."

"If you could be any animal in the world, what animal would you be?"

"That's a tough one. I'd have to say it's a three-way tie between a vulture, a skunk, and a weasel."

"What is your best pickup line?"

"I see all, know all, and love all."

"If you had to give yourself a nickname, what would it be?"

"Oh, that's easy. Sir Monkey-Butt Fudgebucket Scuzzball."

Everyone cracks up. I'm loving the attention.

Large Marge blows her silver whistle. "Okay, Charlene, it's time to identify your mystery date."

"Attention, Norbert Riddle, Nonperson Number L4LUZR-1!" shouts a deep voice from the back of the room.

We all turn around. Sergeant Sergeant marches toward us, clutching his Truthcorder. "You're wanted in Warden Buckner's office. On the double, soldier. Pronto!"

Roger points his finger at me and laughs.

I knew that phony baloney had it out for me. He got me to imitate Loving Leader so Sergeant Sergeant would report me to Bucky. I can't believe I fell for it.

I slowly rise from my seat, put my hands in my pockets, and slump my head.

"I said *pronto*, Riddle,' yells Sergeant Sergeant. "Hup, two, three, four…"

I march across the room and shoot out the door. Sergeant Sergeant tails close behind me. He's following me to make sure I don't try to make a run for it. Not that there's any place for me to run.

Well, I suppose I could locate one of those gonzosauruses, tromp through the forest to Dominic's outdoor workshop, and take off on a helicycle. I could try to fly across Danger Desert. Of course, I'd probably wind up crashing and getting sucked under by the high-speed quicksand, never to be seen again.

With Sergeant Sergeant hot on my heels, I trudge past the watchtower. We cross the meadow, passing the tattered red flag waving atop the flagpole. That's when I notice the ominous Black Box. I nearly have a conniption.

That mysterious box still terrifies me even more than Danger Desert.

After all, I don't have to go anywhere near Danger Desert. I can stay far away from that death trap.

But Bucky Buckner could have me thrown into the Black Box anytime he wants. And who knows what lurks in the darkness?

I picture muck seeping from the walls and sludge dripping from the ceiling.

In the shadows I see stinky alien creatures with

enormous fish heads. Their human hands tug at my gray jumpsuit. They stink like festering garbage.

I imagine myself trapped with throngs of brain-dead intergalactic zombies—all pushing and shoving, coughing and wheezing.

Or maybe the Powder Room really does exist after all—inside the Black Box. The giant disco ball lowers from the ceiling and zaps me with a bright-pink laser beam. *Shazam!* I'm a small pile of bright-pink powder.

Frightened out of my wits, I dash around the mess hall and dart up the steps to Bucky's office.

I burst through the door, close it behind me, and stand with my back against it—to keep any alien creatures outside. Panting, I catch my breath.

Safe at last. Or so I think.

Chapter 37

"How is our new friend coming along?" Bucky Buckner looks me in the eye as he leans back in the tall swivel chair in his office. He folds his arms across his chest and crosses his feet on his glass desk.

That rat fink Roger Payne stands to Bucky's left. He's huffing and puffing. He apparently took a shortcut around back through the woods to beat me here. He combs his fingers through his spiked hair and straightens his hoity-toity ascot. Is that show-off about to get me sent to a barren asteroid?

To Bucky's right stands Howie Rubenstein, the

busybody who never stops snapping photos. His camera dangles around his neck. I wonder how many incriminating photos he's taken of me. My guesstimate? Forty-seven gazillion.

I sit with my hands folded on my lap, staring straight ahead at Bucky. Afraid of whatever he's going to say next. I'm a basket case.

This comfy chair would be a lot more comfortable if I weren't shaking like an imaginary fish caught in an imaginary net.

Scared out of my wits, I clench the arms of my chair, desperately trying to hold myself steady. I'm staring at the large TruthScreen that covers the wall behind Bucky. It's turned off, but I get the awful feeling Bucky is going to press a button on his desk any minute...then Loving Leader will pop up on the screen and thrust his accusing finger at me.

Sitting on a sofa behind me, Sergeant Sergeant taps away at the screen of his Truthcorder. The medals on his jacket clink as he adds more compromising information to my permanent record. My days are definitely numbered. And not just on a calendar.

The door opens and a girl with long blond hair

slips inside and takes a seat on the sofa next to Sergeant Sergeant. Charlene! Is she going to testify against me too? Now I wonder if that whole chopsticks thing was just a trick to get me to talk about my parents. Was she just pretending to like me so I'd join her improv group, drop my guard, and show everyone how different I really am? Has she been working for Loving Leader the entire time?

Bucky removes his sunglasses and narrows his eyes. Realizing I'm gaping at the TruthScreen, he touches a button on his desk. The TruthScreen rises into a long, narrow slot in the ceiling, hiding the monitor from view.

Bucky leans forward. He places his elbows on his glass desk and rubs his palms together. "So, is Norbert thinking outside the box?"

Sergeant Sergeant looks up from his Truthcorder. "Oh yeah!" he exclaims. "Level Five!" He pumps his fist. "Highest score possible!"

Level 5? Now I understand why Sergeant Sergeant has been spying on me. He's been using his Truthcorder to rate the level of my imagination. He definitely works for the Truth Police. No question about it.

But wait, there's no way I'm Level 5. That's way too high.

I mean, Dominic is definitely Level 5. I'm guessing Charlene is Level 4. Roger can't be higher than Level 1. Howie? I'd say Level 2. Which probably makes me Level 3.

What am I thinking? "I'm not any level at all," I want to yell. "I'm not different!"

But I don't say a word. There's no point. Roger set me up, and now Bucky knows for a fact I've only been pretending to be normal. I'm better off keeping my mouth shut so I don't get strike three. Why make things worse? I'm already falling down a bottomless pit.

Drew's words echo in my head. *Think too far outside the box, and you wind up inside the box.*

Scratch that. I'm not falling down a bottomless pit. I'm about to be thrown into the Black Box!

Alone in the eerie darkness.

I can almost feel poison snakes slithering around my ankles and slowly wrapping around my legs.

I picture a headless alien with an eyeball at the end of each of its six fingertips, reaching toward me to see me from different angles and then shoving me into its mouth in the center of its big belly.

Jeez. I'm definitely psyching myself out. Maybe I really do have a Level 5 imagination.

Bucky snaps his fingers. "Charlene, what do you think?"

Charlene nods. "Norbert definitely has the spark."

I'm completely dumbfounded. How could she betray me like this?

Bucky opens a black drawer beneath his glass desk. He reaches inside and holds up a crazy white wig—just like Loving Leader's hair.

Hey, wait a minute. Bucky does look an awful lot like Loving Leader. Maybe he really *is* Loving Leader! Now I get it! His black mustache is fake. I bet he just puts on that wig and peels off the mustache!

"Take him to the Black Box," says Bucky.

I break into a cold sweat.

My worst nightmare is about to come true.

part
two

Chapter 38

Bucky Buckner marches from his office, carrying the crazy wig with him. The door slams closed behind him.

Sergeant Sergeant and Roger close in on me.

"Listen, guys, I think I'll just sit here by myself for a while," I babble. "Really, I'll be fine. No worries. You just go ahead without me."

"Should we tell him?" asks Charlene, rising from the sofa.

"Tell me what?"

Howie zips his lips shut with his two fingertips,

turns an imaginary key, and tosses it aside. "Not yet," he says, forgetting he just zipped his lips shut.

I cling to the arms of the comfy chair and refuse to budge an inch. My ploy doesn't work at all.

Sergeant Sergeant and Roger each grab me by an arm and lift me from the chair. My legs start running in midair, going nowhere fast. Still holding my arms, they escort me outside. Charlene and Howie tag along behind us.

How could I have been such an idiot? Roger got me to incriminate myself with my impression of Loving Leader. Charlene got me to spill the beans on my parents. Howie photographed everything. Sergeant Sergeant documented my every move. Good thing he never figured out that Drew, Sophie, and I broke into his watchtower. That would be strike three for sure. But I still get the horrible feeling Sergeant Sergeant suspects something. He eyes me. I feel the hairs on the back of my neck standing at attention.

I don't know much about the higher power Crazy Swayzee talks to when he says grace, but I beg that higher power to protect me from whatever awaits me in the Black Box. Flesh-eating green slime? An army of skeletons? Zillions of test tubes filled with pink powder?

When we get to the Black Box, Bucky rubs his hands together. He reaches into his pocket for his key chain. It clinks and clatters. Flipping through the keys, he finds a long silver one. He opens the padlock, removes it from the latch, and tugs the door. It creaks open.

I gulp hard. This is it. The end of my freedom. The end of everything.

I look around to catch one last glimpse of the big yellow ball in the bright-blue sky. I see the two moons. The lush green meadow. The red flag waving atop the flagpole.

Good-bye, cruel world. I turn and look into the dark doorway.

Bucky leads the way. With Sergeant Sergeant and Roger Payne still holding my arms, we hike down a dimly lit staircase, descending several flights, followed by our own foreboding shadows. And the occasional flash from Howie Rubenstein's camera.

We traipse through a long tunnel that seems to go on forever, finally opening into a huge, cavernous room.

Using the miniature LaserLight on his key chain,

Bucky locates a heavy lever on the wall. He pulls the handle, and blinding white light fills the room. Bucky throws a second lever, then another and another, switching on more huge bright lights.

I'm seeing stars. Finally my eyes adjust.

Large industrial light fixtures surround a tall chair in the middle of an enormous white room.

I'm about to be interrogated under the harsh bright lights. I just know it. Terrified, I grit my teeth, preparing for the worst.

Sergeant Sergeant and Roger Payne walk me to the center of the light fixtures and seat me in the chair. They stand by my sides like guards, their arms folded across their chests. Sergeant Sergeant presses his Truthcorder against his medals.

Howie Rubenstein circles around the room, snapping photographs of me surrounded by bright lights and intimidating Astro-Nuts. Charlene drills her eyes into mine.

I'm about to burst into tears, but I decide to be brave and hold them back.

Bucky steps in front of me and holds up the white wig, dangling it in my face.

THE CENTER OF ATTENTION

No one says a word.

"What's this all about?" I plead. "Are you going to make an example out of me?"

Bucky grimaces with wry amusement.

I look into his dark sunglasses, unable to see his eyes. "You're Loving Leader, aren't you?"

Chapter 39

Bucky Buckner bursts into wild laughter. He actually cackles.

Everyone else cracks up too. They're all hooting and howling.

Even Sergeant Sergeant. Of course, it's hard to tell if Sergeant Sergeant's chuckles are genuine. He could be laughing just to suck up to Bucky.

I have no idea why everyone's laughing at me.

"What's so funny?" I ask.

Bucky catches his breath and wipes the tears from his eyes. That's how hard he's been laughing at me. "Norbert, you've got quite the imagination."

"No, I really don't," I lie. "I don't have any imagination. I swear it. I'm not different at all. I'm nothing but a pea-brained chowderhead. A dim-witted goofball. Just your run-of-the-mill nincompoop. Send me home. Please, I beg you. Send me back to Earth."

"Norbert, this isn't an interrogation chamber. I'm not Loving Leader."

"Sure, you're not."

"Norbert, this wig is for *you.*" He holds up the crazy white hairpiece.

"For me?"

"Yes, so you can do your impression of Loving Leader." He tosses the wig to me.

I catch it. "So you want me to incriminate myself so you can lock me up in this Black Box forever. Thanks, but no thanks." I toss the wig back to him.

"Norbert, you don't understand. This Black Box is our brand-new television production studio."

Now I'm totally confused. "What are you talking about? Isn't the Black Box some sort of punishment? You told me there was something *very* different and *very* dangerous in here."

Bucky shakes his head. "No, Norbert. That was

just my way to stop you—a very curious young man—from breaking in here and discovering our secret project, which does happen to be *very* different and *very* dangerous."

I never noticed Howie leave the room, but he returns, rolling a large television camera.

Charlene steps forward. "We've built this top secret television production studio so we can create our own television show."

"Loving Leader thinks Astro-Nuts Camp is a prison where creative people are treated like lunatics," says Bucky. "But it's not. It's a place where creativity is nurtured, encouraged, and celebrated. And the beauty is, Loving Leader keeps sending us the best and brightest, the most talented kids on Earth. Kids like you."

I'm touched, but I'm still suspicious. "But who's going to watch this television show?"

"Everyone on Zorquat Three. We're going to set up big screens."

"Where did you get all this equipment?" I ask.

Bucky points to three large metallic crates at the back of the room. "When Grissom delivered you to Zorquat Three aboard that spaceship, he also brought those. He smuggles us whatever we need from Earth."

"But why didn't you just tell me all this when I got here?"

"We had to make sure you weren't a spy for the Truth Police."

Good thing no one caught me in the watchtower. I sneak a glance at Sergeant Sergeant. Yeah, he's still messing with his Truthcorder and occasionally gazing at Charlene. There's no way I'll ever trust that guy.

Bucky steps over to a tall board covered with a white sheet. "And the name of our television show is…" He tugs off the sheet, revealing a colorful stage set painted with the word ASTRO-NUTS!

Everyone in the room cheers. Except me.

I'm totally stunned by all this. "What about the barren asteroid?" I ask. "Is that bogus too?"

"No, that's real," says Bucky. "If you refuse to participate here, you get sent up there. So what do you say, Norbert? We really want you to be a big part of this."

Chapter 40

burst into tears. Weird reaction, I know.

I'm totally relieved to know that nothing scary whatsoever looms inside the Black Box. I'm also really flattered that everyone wants me to be a part of the television show. But I don't want to spend the rest of my life on Zorquat 3. I want to find my parents.

Bucky looks deeply concerned. He pulls me aside. "Norbert, what's wrong? I thought this would make you happy."

I'm afraid to tell Bucky the truth, petrified he'll

give me strike three and send me to the barren asteroid.

Bucky raises his eyebrows. "Seriously, what's troubling you? Whatever it is, I'm sure we can work it out."

I take a deep breath. "I don't want to work on a television show here on Zorquat Three," I confess. "I want to go home. Please, Bucky, let me go back to Earth. I'm begging you." Tears stream down my cheeks.

Bucky folds his arms across his chest. He peers into my eyes and frowns. His mustache twitches.

I'm about to get strike three. I just know it.

I tremble, desperately trying to hold myself together.

Bucky sighs. "All right, Norbert, I'll tell you what. Let's do this differently. If you agree to run this television show, and if it's really funny and a big hit with all the other Astro-Nuts, the next time Grissom lands here in his spaceship, I'll sneak you back to Earth."

"For real?"

Bucky nods. "That's a promise. Do we have a deal?"

I wipe the tears from my eyes. I hold out my little finger. "Pinky swear?"

Bucky laughs. And then shakes my pinky with his.

Hope at last!

Now all I've got to do is pull off the impossible.

To tell you the truth, I'm even more terrified than ever. After all, I've never run a television show before.

The next day, at our first meeting in the Black Box, Large Marge notices me trembling. "What's wrong, Norbert?"

"I have no idea what I'm doing," I say. "I'm a nervous wreck."

"Nervousness and excitement are the exact same feeling," she says.

"I don't understand. How can that be?"

"Nervous is negative. Excited is positive. Instead of telling yourself, 'I'm nervous,' tell yourself, 'I'm excited.' Flipping nervousness on its head completely changes your attitude."

"But if the show bombs, Bucky will refuse to ever send me home."

"Stop what-iffing."

"What-whatting?"

"Asking yourself 'what if' all the time, like you did with the Black Box. '*What if* the Black Box is used for solitary confinement?' '*What if* the Black Box is filled with horrible creatures?' '*What if* I get locked in the Black Box?' You're creating all sorts of ridiculous scenarios in your mind and then worrying about them until you completely freak yourself out. Stop scaring yourself. Stick with what is."

She kisses me on the forehead Now I know why everyone calls her Large Marge. She has a really big heart.

Bucky wheels a giant backdrop into the room. It looks like a huge canvas splattered by paint balloons, with bursts of purple, yellow, green, orange, blue, and red paint I have to admit, it looks really cool. Outrageous, but definitely cool.

"Now remember," says Bucky. "There are no rules. You can do whatever you want, Norbert—as long as it's funny."

"I'll do my best. In fact, I'll do better than my best. On second thought, I don't think that's humanly possible. I can't do better than my best. It's already my best."

Charlene laughs.

"Don't let me down," says Bucky. He gives me a big thumbs-up and skedaddles from the room.

Charlene smiles at me. I smile back at her. She winks at me. I wink back at her.

I decide to pop the question. No, not marriage... I'm only twelve. "So why do you eat only with chopsticks?" I ask.

"Because I can."

"That's it? That's your entire explanation?"

"On Earth, eating with chopsticks is illegal. Loving Leader permits only forks, spoons, and knives. But eating with chopsticks is a lot more fun."

"Aren't they hard to use?"

"It just takes practice, like improv. Would you like me to teach you?"

My heart melts. I give her a soft peck on the cheek.

"Give it a rest," says Sergeant Sergeant. "Don't forget, I've still got my eyes on you."

Little does he know, I've got my eyes on him, too.

Chapter 41

I decide to take the bull by the horns. Even though there is no bull.

What am I saying? There's plenty of bull. Mostly from Roger Payne.

Roger's a real doozy. He's so full of himself I'm surprised he doesn't explode. He's bossing everyone around, telling everyone what to do. "Move this over there! Move that over here!"

While Roger is busy playing the role of stage manager, I recruit Drew to help write sketches for the show. I mean, if anyone can spew wild ideas, it's Drew. We're also going to need live music. Some kind of band. So I invite Sophie to be our bandleader and ask her to enlist some of her talented musician friends. I take Drew and Sophie aside and let them both in on my secret plan to use this whole television production to my advantage.

"Yeah, but how are we going to get our hands on the Truthcorder without Sergeant Sergeant noticing?" asks Drew, eager to help.

"Don't worry." I tap my forehead with my index finger. "I have an idea."

"Careful," says Sophie. "That's one of the three deadly warning signs of imagination."

We all crack up.

"Speaking of ideas, I've got a great idea for the show," says Drew. "Picture a giant white room. Just like this one. There's a raised dance floor, lit from underneath, like in a nightclub. A giant mirrored disco ball hangs from the ceiling. Guards drag Roger, dressed like a prisoner, to the middle of the dance floor. At the flick of a switch, the disco ball lowers from the ceiling and zaps him with a bright-pink laser beam. *Poof!* He's turned into a small pile of—"

"Pink powder."

"How'd you know?"

"You told me all about the Powder Room back on Earth when we were in that prison cell together. It's been haunting me ever since."

"Yeah, I'm really sorry I put all those scary thoughts in your head. I was just sharing some of my wild ideas."

"Well, let's see if we can turn that idea into a funny sketch somehow."

Sophie ushers in a group of her musician friends. They're lugging all sorts of musical instruments.

Keisha rolls in the brass kettle gongs. *Bing-a-bang-a-bing-a-boing!*

Farley Chung assembles the clanging bars. *Clinkity clank clonkity clank!*

Jasmine starts thumping the conga drums. *Whump thump whumpity thump!*

Zach sets up the snakelike horn and blows into the mouthpiece. *Bwappa bwah bwah bwap!*

"You wanted to see me, partner?" Crazy Swayzee ambles over in his snakeskin boots, his thumbs stuck in his front pockets. "What can I do you for?"

I tell Swayzee my plans for the television show. "I

really love the Astro-Nuts song you sang at the Love Fest the other night."

"Well, that's mighty nice of you to say so."

"Would you sing it on the show as the opening theme song?"

"Gadzooks! It's one thing to sing at the Love Fest. It's a whole 'nother can of worms to sing on some highfalutin television show."

"Hold everything!" Roger bursts onto the set and storms toward us. "Just what do you think you're doing, Norbert?" Red smoke may as well be streaming from his ears. "Who do you think you are? I should be the one running this show. Not you!"

ROGER SURE KNOWS HOW TO ACT...
LIKE A TWO-YEAR-OLD.

"Huh? There must be some misunderstanding."

"Oh, there's a misunderstanding, all right. Norbert Riddle, I challenge you to a duel!" Roger jumps into a starting fencing position and thrusts his right hand forward, brandishing an imaginary fencing sword. "En garde!"

"Seriously? A duel with pretend swords?"

"No," replies Roger. "A battle of wits."

Chapter 42

Large Marge agrees to referee the battle of wits between Roger and me, in the form of an improv game.

If I lose this game, Roger gets to run the television show and I lose my one-way ticket home. I'm nervous beyond belief. I can barely breathe.

We play rock-paper-scissors to determine who will choose the game. Roger wins and picks Expert Challenge, the game where you pretend to be an expert on a specific topic. It's Roger's specialty.

A wave of panic sweeps over me as we walk onto

a stage that's been set up in the room. I force myself to take a deep breath.

Large Marge turns to the audience. "All right, can someone please suggest an article of clothing?"

"A cowboy hat," yells Tex Swayzee. He tips the hat on his head.

"Sparkly silver shoes," shouts Sophie.

"Socks," shouts Farley Chung.

"All right, Roger and Norbert, you have three minutes to demonstrate which one of you is the world's leading expert on..." Large Marge raises the whistle to her lips. *"Socks!"*

She blows her silver whistle.

Roger clasps his jacket lapels. "Socks are usually worn on people's feet. They're an article of clothing available in pairs. Just like pants. You can wear a pair of socks, and you can wear a pair of pants."

I step forward. "Challenge! A pair of socks consists of two socks—two separate garments. A pair of pants is one garment."

"Correct!" says Large Marge. "The floor goes to Norbert. You may continue!"

I raise my finger to punctuate the air. "Socks come in all different colors, designs, and fabrics. There are fuzzy socks, argyle socks, polka-dot socks, and red socks. There's no shortage of socks!"

"Challenge!" yells Roger. "I have a shortage of socks. I'm *always* losing socks. I have a whole bunch of single socks that have lost their matching sock. Therefore, I have a shortage of socks."

Large Marge nods in agreement. "Correct! Roger gets the floor. Please continue!"

"When you lose socks, you can still mix and match your remaining socks. You can wear a fuzzy sock with an argyle sock. Or a polka-dot sock with a red sock. Another type of sock is a tube sock. Tube socks tend to be higher than regular socks."

I wave my hands in protest. "Challenge! Not if the regular socks are on top of a mountain, and the tube socks are in a valley!"

"Correct!" says Large Marge. "Then the regular socks would definitely be higher than the tube socks. Norbert, take the floor!"

I hesitate for a split second, not sure what to say next. I start sweating. Profusely.

Then it hits me. "If you're going to wear socks on top of a mountain, you should wear thick, heavy socks to keep your feet warm."

Roger sneers. "Challenge! If you're on top of a mountain on a hot summer day, you may not want to wear any socks at all."

"That's right!" agrees Large Marge. "Roger! Proceed!"

"If you don't want to wear socks, you can wear sandals. You can also wear socks *with* sandals. But don't wear socks with sandals that separate your toes, like flip-flops. Unless you have toe socks. Toe socks are like gloves for your feet that give each one of your toes its own little sock. Toe socks keep your feet warmer than other socks."

I wave my arms. "Challenge! Wearing two pairs of socks keeps your feet much warmer than toe socks."

Large Marge nods. "How true! Norbert, continue, if you please."

"And wearing three pairs of socks keeps your feet warmer than two pairs of socks. Of course, wearing too many pairs of socks makes it difficult to fit your feet into your shoes."

"Challenge!" Roger clenches his fists. "Not if your shoes are clown shoes."

The audience laughs and cheers.

Large Marge chuckles. "Indeed! Roger, time is running out. Go ahead."

"Clown shoes are very big shoes. So you can wear any size socks you wish. You can wear small socks, medium socks, large socks, or even extra-large socks. Socks are just like people. They come in all shapes and sizes."

"Challenge!" I wag my finger. "I'm not like a sock at all. You can't wear me on your feet." Did I just say something horribly stupid? Did I just blow my free trip home?

Large Marge tilts her head and looks at me like I just said something completely absurd. Then she raises her eyebrows. "I can't argue with that! Carry on, Norbert!"

"Socks can also be worn on your hands. If you don't have any gloves, you can keep your hands warm by wearing socks on them. Or you can use a sock on your hand as a puppet." I hold up my hand like a puppet and make it talk. "Hello, I'm a puppet. How are you today?"

I look to the audience. Charlene is laughing hysterically.

"Challenge!" yells Roger. "That's not a sock puppet. That's just his hand."

"Correct!" says Large Marge.

"Challenge!" I yell. I pull a shoe off my foot, remove my sock, and pull it over my hand. I make my sock puppet talk. "Hello, everybody! I'm going to knock your socks off!"

The crowd applauds and cheers.

Large Marge blows her whistle. "And our time's up! Now, who will our winner be?"

Chapter 43

The room goes totally silent. Except for the snapping of Howie Rubenstein's camera.

Everyone in the audience stares at us. Drew. Sophie. Charlene. Crazy Swayzee. Dominic and Farley. Keisha, Jasmine, and Zach. And most important of all, Bucky Buckner. I feel their eyeballs ricocheting between Roger and me.

Sergeant Sergeant stands near the back wall, glued to his Truthcorder. Tapping away as usual.

My heart races. My stomach feels like it's tied in knots. Or maybe that's my small intestine.

Large Marge steps between us. "To determine our

winner, we're going to use our applause meter." She holds her hand above Roger's head. "Applaud if you think the winner of our Expert Challenge is Roger Payne."

The kids applaud loudly. It's kind of overwhelming.

Roger smiles, pumps his fist, and takes a bow. He looks to me and grins smugly. He winks at Charlene.

I'm just standing there. My throat goes dry. Did I lose?

"All right, settle down." Large Marge steps closer to me. She holds her hand above my head. "Now applaud if you think the winner of our Expert Challenge is Norbert Riddle."

The room explodes with applause. Then hoots and hollers! Everyone starts stomping their feet.

"And we have a winner!" announces Large Marge. She grabs my hand and raises it in the air. "It's official. Norbert Riddle will run *Astro-Nuts*."

I can't believe it! What a relief!

Everyone starts chanting, "Norbert! Norbert! Norbert!"

In the audience Sophie gives Drew a high five.

Charlene blows me a kiss. Bucky Buckner gives me two thumbs-ups. Even Sergeant Sergeant looks up from his Truthcorder for a second.

Roger doesn't seem too happy. His face goes completely sour. He puts his hands in his pockets and lowers his head. The guy looks really pathetic.

I reach out to shake his hand. I'm willing to let bygones be bygones. "Good game," I say. "You're a worthy opponent."

But Roger refuses to shake hands. "Oh, put a sock in it!" he says. "I quit."

Wow. Talk about a poor sport.

Defeated, Roger turns his back on me. He tromps off into the wings—the side of the stage that the audience can't see.

I feel sorry for the guy. I mean, he may be a poser and a bit of a snob (okay, make that a *huge* snob), but I didn't mean to humiliate him. Or hurt his feelings in any way.

Okay, he did try to steal my job running the show. But I'm sure I'd feel the same way if some funny new kid came along. I'd probably feel jealous and spiteful, just like Roger does.

No, that's not true at all. I wouldn't be jealous, and I'd never be nasty. I'd be totally supportive and work together so we could learn from each other, stand on each other's shoulders, and become even funnier.

So maybe Roger really is a jerk. A talented jerk. But a jerk nonetheless.

But that doesn't mean I have to be a jerk too. I can take the high road.

I decide to chase after Roger.

Too late. Everyone leaps to the stage, circles around me, and lifts me onto their shoulders. They parade me around the room, cheering and chanting, "Norbert! Norbert! Norbert!" They really go crazy. It feels incredible. Unbelievable. Sensational.

When they finally put me down and finish congratulating me, I look around backstage for Roger, but he's long gone. I should be feeling on top of the world. Instead I feel horrible.

I return to unit 16. Roger is lying on his bunk. His face is buried in his pillow. He's obviously not taking defeat well.

I sit down on the bunk next to his. "Hey, Roger, listen, I'm really sorry you feel this way."

"No, you're not," he mutters.

"Yes, I really am. From the first time I watched you play Yay!/Boo! against Charlene, I thought you were amazingly funny and talented. Then we played Yay!/Boo! against each other, and I thought, 'Wow, what a clever guy.' From day one I've laughed at your jokes. Please don't quit the *Astro-Nuts* show. I want you and Charlene to cohost the fake news segment."

Roger sits up. "You really mean that? You're not just pulling my leg, are you?"

"I want you to star in the rest of the show too. We really need you."

Roger doesn't say anything for a long time. He just sinks his head back into his pillow. "Go away," he mumbles. "You don't deserve to have someone as talented as me in your show." The pillow muffles his voice.

I'm pretty sure he's crying.

I decide I'd better leave Roger alone. I get up from the bunk and go back to the Black Box.

If Roger doesn't want to be in the show, that's his call. At least I tried. I really did mean everything I said.

There's only one problem.

I'm not exactly sure how to pull off the show without him.

Chapter 44

In case you haven't noticed, from the moment I arrived on Zorquat 3, I haven't exactly been thrilled to be here. All I've wanted to do is go home. And find my parents. More than anything else in the world.

But now that Bucky has offered me the chance to go home, I'm determined to make this television show the funniest show ever. Sure, there's a lot of pressure, but it's also a lot of fun. I'm actually having the time of my life, if you really want to know the truth. Everyone is creative and imaginative and full of great ideas. We make one another laugh all day long.

To be honest, I've never laughed so much in my entire life. I wouldn't mind doing this all the time. Well, not *all* the time. Occasionally I like to sleep.

We do everything ourselves—write the scripts, build and paint the sets, create the costumes. And then we rehearse, rehearse, rehearse. You can almost taste the excitement as we get everything ready for our first show. What does excitement taste like? A lot better than gruel, that's all I can say.

Whenever we get stuck for an idea, Large Marge runs an improv game to free our imaginations. It sounds crazy, but playing a quick round of Yay!/Boo! or Expert Challenge helps us think outside the box and come up with fresh material.

Everyone from our improv group is having a blast at rehearsals. Charlene, Keisha, Jasmine, Zach... everyone except Roger. That's because he's not here. He's still throwing a kissy fit.

I put Farley Chung in charge of costumes. He's a natural fit. No pun intended. I've never met anyone who loves clothes as much as Farley. He knows exactly what each character in every sketch should be wearing.

I ask Farley what I should wear when I play Loving Leader.

"Your gray jumpsuit, of course," he says. "And the white wig. Don't forget the white wig."

Farley knows his stuff.

So does Howie Rubenstein. As far as cameras go, that is. Not wardrobe. That's why I assigned Howie to operate the television camera. He really knows cameras. They just seem to click.

I put Dominic Garcia in charge of running the control room. That's the big room filled with all sorts of whatchamacallits. Mixers, consoles, monitors... all that junk.

There's enough state-of-the-art equipment in there to launch a rocket back to Earth. Too bad we don't have our own rocket.

In private I ask Dominic to secretly prepare the equipment in the control room to hack into Sergeant Sergeant's Truthcorder. "When someone hands you the Truthcorder, look up my permanent record and find out where my parents are."

"But how do you plan to get your hands on it?" asks Dominic.

"Just leave that to me."

"What if you get caught?"

"I guess that will go in my permanent record—as strike three. Let's just say I'll try my best to not let that happen."

I return to the stage and take a seat in the audience, and listen to Sophie and her band practice. They plunk gongs, clang bells, and thump drums. They sound great.

Suddenly the stage opens and in walks Crazy Swayzee, carrying his Wazooper. He straps the lop-sided electric guitar around his neck and howls like a total madman.

The band stops. Dead silence.

"I decided to join your whoop-de-do after all," says Swayzee. "And I brought along someone else who's had a change of heart."

From behind the partition steps someone with spiked hair and a tweed jacket. The ascot is gone.

Roger seems a lot less full of himself. Like someone who's been knocked down a few pegs. It turns out Bucky had a little talk with him. Something about barren asteroids.

Roger steps over to greet me. "Listen, Norbert, I'm really sorry we started off on the wrong foot."

"You mean, the foot you used to trip me?"

Roger nods. "I do love your impression of Loving Leader. I'm the one who told Bucky about it so he'd invite you to join the show. I'm sorry I've been such a…"

"Phony baloney?"

"If your offer is still good, I'd really like to cohost the fake news. If you still want me."

I offer Roger my hand.

This time he shakes it.

Large Marge reminds us the *Astro-Nuts* show will be broadcast to everyone on planet Zorquat 3. Now I'm incredibly nervous.

"What if I do a terrible job? What if we bomb? What if everyone hates it?"

"Stop what-iffing." says Large Marge.

"But what if I'm right?"

Chapter 45

Large Marge stands next to the television camera operated by Howie Rubenstein. "Ten seconds till showtime," she says.

In the amphitheater hundreds of Astro-Nuts sit in the bleachers, watching an enormous Truth-Screen that Dominic Garcia hacked so it only receives shows broadcast on Zorquat 3. Hundreds more Astro-Nuts sit on benches in the mess hall, facing another modified TruthScreen. And of course, dozens of kids make up the live audience inside the Black Box.

My heart pounds. I want to run away and hide. Instead I take a deep breath. Here goes whatever.

Large Marge waves her hand. The green light on the television camera flashes. *Astro-Nuts* is off and running! Now we either sink or swim.

Bucky Buckner announces, "And now an important message from His Royal Eminence, the All-Knowing Supreme Grand Pooh-Bah and All-Around Excellent Ruler of Earth, the great and powerful Loving Leader!"

I stand at a lectern, wearing my gray jumpsuit and the crazy wig of white hair.

The audience cracks up and applauds. They're into it. The stage is set. Now I just have to deliver.

"My fellow earthlings," I say. "The time to conform is now. Or possibly tomorrow. But mostly now. Because tomorrow, today will be yesterday, and tomorrow will be today. The truth is: Tomorrow never comes. It is always today. Tomorrow is a lie. A dangerous lie blocking our path to a successful future. Yes, my fellow earthlings, we must declare war on tomorrow. But not today."

The audience chuckles. I stare at the crowd. I'm

starting to sweat. The chuckles suddenly turn into loud laughter and applause. I'm a hit. Now I just have to keep it up.

"Today we must win the war against creativity. Unfortunately, our enemies are creative. They think up clever ideas that threaten our mediocrity. Their minds are diseased, like mine. That's why we can never tolerate imaginative people. We must never tolerate tolerance, either. Tolerance is intolerable. Imagine no imaginative people! Rebel against rebellion! Yes, blind obedience will set you free!"

The audience goes wild. They're laughing out loud and applauding like crazy. "I am not a dictator. I'm your friend. A friend with absolute power and total control. I love ruling over you. Because you, my fellow earthlings, are the best people on Earth. I love telling you how to live your lives. I love ordering you to believe whatever I say. I love striking fear into your hearts, imprisoning nonconformists, and banishing nonpersons to the other side of the universe. After all, there is nothing to fear but those who fear nothing!

"Remember, Loving Leader sees London, Loving Leader sees France, Loving Leader sees your underpants."

I hold up two fingers to make the letter L—for "loser."

The audience cheers. They stand up to applaud. They really let it rip. It's the most hysterical impression of Loving Leader I've ever done. I'm a sensation!

The camera zooms in on my face. "And live from Zorquat Three in the Orion Nebula, it's *Astro-Nuts*!"

Sophie and the Astro-Nuts Band start banging

their funky kettles, chimes, and gongs. In the control room, Dominic Garcia cuts to the opening credits. We see Drew's caricatures of the entire cast. Bucky Buckner stands in the wings and narrates into a microphone.

"Starring the Astro-Nuts! Charlene Gordon, Drew Weaver, Roger Payne, Farley Chung, Norbert Riddle, Sophie Singer, Sergeant Sergeant, and the Astro-Nuts Band! Tonight's musical guest: Crazy Tex Swayzee. And me—your announcer—Bucky Buckner!"

Crazy Swayzee steps up to a microphone, looks to the ceiling, and howls like a total madman. Then he starts strumming that strange-looking eleven-stringed Wazooper. The audience claps to the beat. He sings a new version of his Astro-Nuts song. It's... different and dangerous!

Chapter 46

After the opening credits we do a fake commercial.

Wearing a gray jumpsuit, Roger sits at a kitchen table in a tiny gray kitchen with gray wallpaper.

Charlene Gordon, wearing a gray apron over her gray jumpsuit, slops a ladle of gruel in a small gray bowl and sets it on the table in front of Roger.

"Here's your morning gruel, dear," she says.

Roger puts down his newspaper. "Gruel, gruel, gruel. I'm sick of gruel. Having to eat gruel three times a day is driving me completely nuts!"

"Did someone say 'nuts'?" Farley Chung, wearing a tight-fitting space suit and a Viking helmet, pops into the kitchen, lowered from the ceiling by wires. He holds a box of cereal.

Charlene looks astonished. "Who are you?"

Farley spins in place on his wires and bounces around the small room. "Nutty for Astro-Nuts!"

Roger and Charlene each try a bowl of Astro-Nuts cereal. They start bouncing around the room too.

Bucky Buckner announces, "Astro-Nuts cereal! With real nuts! Part of an unbalanced breakfast. For people who think outside the box. *Cereal* box, that is!"

"Wow!" says Roger. "Astro-Nuts are really nuts!"

Charlene holds the cereal box up to the camera. "Yeah, and now so are we!"

"I'm nutty for Astro-Nuts!" Farley gets pulled up from the set like he's bouncing back into outer space.

Meanwhile, backstage, it's time to put my plan into action.

I race back over to the dressing rooms and knock on the door with Sergeant Sergeant's name on it. (Actually, the sign says SARGE[2].)

Sergeant Sergeant opens the door, clutching his Truthcorder. He's dressed in a gray jumpsuit with a black wig to look like my mean, old middle school teacher. The makeup on his face makes him look all wrinkled like a prune. Just like Mrs. Hurlbutt.

I cast Sergeant Sergeant to play the part of Mrs.

Hurlbutt in the next sketch for two reasons. One, he's just as nasty as Mrs. Hurlbutt. But more importantly, I need to divert his attention. "We're on in thirty seconds," I tell him.

We walk over to the set and take our places. It's a classroom, just like the one back home in Middle School Number 1022, Region 154. The walls are painted gray. The sky painted on the background behind the windows is gray. To play students, the other actors and I wear the exact same gray jumpsuits.

I take a seat at a school desk. Sergeant Sergeant sits behind the teacher's desk at the head of the classroom. I signal Drew, standing in the wings, by touching the tip of my nose with my index finger.

Drew leaps onto the set and races over to the teacher's desk.

Sergeant Sergeant looks up, surprised.

"You better let me take that," says Drew, pointing to the Truthcorder in Sergeant Sergeant's grip. "I'll keep it backstage during your sketch. We don't want to see that on camera."

Sergeant Sergeant gapes at him. His eyebrows twitch. "I'll just put it in one of these drawers."

"They're all locked shut," says Drew. That is a bold lie. But you have to give Drew credit. He's pretty quick on his feet. "We're on in ten seconds."

Sergeant Sergeant doesn't have time to check all the drawers. He just hands over the Truthcorder.

Drew runs backstage. He's got only six minutes.

The clock is running.

Chapter 47

Dressed as Mrs. Hurlbutt, Sergeant Sergeant picks up the flügelhorn sitting on the teacher's desk and blasts "Twinkle, Twinkle, Little Star." *Bwaah bwaah blooot blooot blurp blurp blooot!*

"Good morning, class, and welcome to Middle School Number 1022," says Sergeant Sergeant. "I'm your teacher, Mrs. Hurlbutt."

The audience laughs.

I raise my hand. "I'm sorry, could you repeat that?"

"Mrs. Hurlbutt!"

The whole audience cracks up.

"Okay, class, that's enough. Now rise for the pledge."

The entire class responds: "Yes, Mrs. Hurlbutt!"

The audience starts hooting like crazy.

We all stand at attention and face the Truth-Screen at the front of the classroom. Sergeant Sergeant's character, Mrs. Hurlbutt, holds up two fingers to make the letter *V*. "Does anyone know what the letter *V* stands for?"

I raise my hand again. "Vomit," I say.

Hysterical laughter.

We recite the pledge. "I pledge convenience to Shoving Leaper of the Excited Snake of Mirth, and to the stomach on glitch shake hands, one basement blunder fragrance, invisible, with trickery and jaundice play ball."

(I recited the Pledge of Subservience into Dominic's divergent gibberish transducer, and that's how his gizmo translated the words.)

The audience goes wild.

In unison, we plop back down at our school desks. I prop my elbow on my desk, rest my head in my hand, and gaze out the window at the gray clouds painted on the gray sky on the background.

"You there!" shouts Sergeant Sergeant as Mrs. Hurlbutt. "You, staring out the window! Norbert Riddle, Person Number L4LUZR-1."

I pretend to be startled. I almost fall out of my chair.

The audience laughs.

I turn my head from the window and look at Mrs. Hurlbutt. Standing in front of my desk, she (Sergeant Sergeant) raises the flügelhorn to her lips. She blasts "Twinkle, Twinkle, Little Star" directly in my face.

"Are you daydreaming?" yells Mrs. Hurlbutt. "Daydreaming is one of the three deadly warning signs of imagination."

"And what are the other two warning signs?" I ask.

"Thinking of an idea," says Mrs. Hurlbutt.

"And the third?"

Mrs. Hurlbutt grins. Some of Sergeant Sergeant's teeth are blackened to look missing. "I, uh…I don't remember."

Flashing red lights drop from the ceiling and start whirling. Sirens start wailing. Farley and Roger—dressed as Truth Police—burst through the door. They point big laser guns at Mrs. Hurlbutt. Not real laser guns. Just stage props.

"You're under arrest," says Farley.

"Me? What for?" asks Mrs. Hurlbutt. "I'm not different, I'm not dangerous, and I'm not daydreaming."

"No, you're just despicable." Roger slaps handcuffs on Mrs. Hurlbutt's wrists. "You're a despicable teacher and a despicable human being, and you don't know the third deadly warning sign of imagination. That's just…despicable!"

"Tell me, please," says Mrs. Hurlbutt. "What is the third warning sign? I'm curious to know."

"That's it!" says Farley. "Curiosity!"

"Guilty as charged!" says Roger.

The Truth Police drag her in handcuffs from the classroom.

I grab the flügelhorn and play "Twinkle, Twinkle, Little Star."

Bwaah bwaah blooot blooot blurp blurp blooot!

Thunderous applause.

The second we finish the sketch, I run backstage, still holding the flügelhorn.

Drew finds me. "Big problem," he says. "I gave the Truthcorder to Dominic, just like you told me. But he can't hack into it."

We race over to the control room. "What's wrong?" I ask.

"This isn't working like it's supposed to," says Dominic.

Yellow wires run from Sergeant Sergeant's Truthcorder to a thingamadoodle. Green wires snake up a tall flumadiddle. Pink wires plug into the deely-bopper.

Now I'm really getting worried. "What seems to be the problem?"

"I can't get past the password screen," says Dominic. "I'm locked out."

"The sketch just ended. We better give up and get the Truthcorder back to Sergeant Sergeant before he realizes something's up. I don't want you to get caught."

"Just stall him for three more minutes."

My heart is beating like one of those crazy drums. "Okay, three minutes."

I have no idea how I'm going to pull that off.

Chapter 48

Drew and I hunt feverishly around backstage for Sergeant Sergeant while the show continues. I'm starting to panic because I have to change costumes and be back onstage for another sketch right after the fake news segment.

"And now it's *Astro-Nuts News*," announces Bucky Buckner. "Nutty news for news nuts."

The audience applauds.

Charlene sits behind a news desk onstage, holds a sheaf of papers, and looks directly into the camera. Her long blond hair is in a bun, held in place with chopsticks. "Good evening. I'm Charlene Gordon."

"And I'm Roger Payne." He sits next to Charlene at the news desk, holding his own stack of papers.

Meanwhile, backstage, Drew and I find Sergeant Sergeant, still dressed in his Mrs. Hurlbutt costume. His wrists remain handcuffed behind his back.

Farley kneels behind him, holding a brass key. He's about to unlock the handcuffs.

Drew races over to them. "Let me help you with that." He grabs the key from Farley.

Farley shrugs and steps back.

Onstage, Charlene says, "Tonight's top story: The citizens of Earth started dancing in the streets today when Loving Leader announced that elections will be held for a new All-Knowing Eternal Excellency. The celebration ended abruptly when it was learned that Loving Leader is running for reelection and will be the only name on the ballot."

The crowd roars with laughter.

Backstage, Drew kneels behind Sergeant Sergeant and fiddles with the key. "You did a great job, Sarge," he says. "Hysterical. Absolutely hysterical. Wasn't he hysterical, Norbert?"

"Hysterical," I say.

"Thank you," says Sergeant Sergeant. "Now get me out of these handcuffs!"

"In a jiffy." Drew turns his head to me and winks.

He fidgets with the key. Pretending to try to open the handcuffs. "This key doesn't seem to work," he says. "Norbert, are you sure this is the right key?"

I play along. "Pretty sure."

"Get me out of these things," snaps Sergeant Sergeant.

Sophie skirts around the partition and grabs the flügelhorn from me. "The band needs this for the next sketch coming up in a few minutes. You better get ready. You're in it, remember?"

She suddenly notices Drew fiddling with the handcuff key. "What's going on?" she asks.

I take Sophie aside. "We're stalling to buy Dominic more time to hack into the Truthcorder without the password. He's still locked out."

"I know the password."

"Say what?" I grab her by the hand. I turn to Drew

and Sergeant Sergeant. "Sophie and I are going to go look for another key. We'll be right back."

Drew continues pretending to turn the key in the handcuffs that refuse to open. Fortunately, Sergeant Sergeant can't see what's going on behind his back.

Sophie and I rush into the control room. Dominic holds the Truthcorder in his hands. He's switching the yellow wires with the green wires. Beads of sweat race down his forehead.

"Let me see that," says Sophie. She hands the flügelhorn to me, grabs the Truthcorder from Dominic, and taps the screen, entering a code. *Bweep bweep bwoop bwoop bwaap bwapp bwoop!*

The Truthcorder password screen opens. Magically.

Dominic's mouth drops open. "I don't understand. How'd you know the password?"

"Didn't you hear the song when I punched in the numbers? It's 'Twinkle, Twinkle, Little Star.' The musical notes match the numbers on the keypad."

In an instant Dominic downloads everything from the Truthcorder. He taps the screen, locks it shut again, and hands me the device.

I race backstage and slip the Truthcorder to Drew. He turns the key, and the handcuffs pop open. Sergeant Sergeant is set free. He rubs his sore wrists.

Drew hands him the Truthcorder.

We did it!

Or so I think.

Chapter 49

Large Marge calls me to the stage. It's time for the next sketch, starring Roger and yours truly. She helps me change into a Truth Police costume at super-duper-hyper-turbo-zippo-speed.

On a giant white set, a bunch of Astro-Nuts stand frozen in various dance poses on a raised dance floor, lit from underneath. On the wall a sign made from a zillion tiny lightbulbs reads THE POWDER ROOM. A huge, mirrored disco ball hangs from the ceiling.

I usher Roger to the center of the dance floor. He's dressed as a prisoner in a gray jumpsuit.

"Now, Roger, you've been deemed different and dangerous because you love to dance. Is that a fact?"

"Oh, yes, I love to dance!"

"Well, you're in luck, Roger, because here in the Powder Room, you and all these other nonpersons can dance to your heart's content."

"Great!"

"There's just one itsy-bitsy rule. You can dance all you want, but you have to keep both feet on this star." I point to a large, five-pointed star painted in the center of the dance floor. "Do you promise to do that?"

"Yes, yes! I love to dance."

"Terrific. Just keep your feet on the star. Now I'll start the music!" I hold up a remote control and press a button.

Sophie and the Astro-Nuts Band clang their gongs, bang their drums, and blow the flügelhorn—making wild dance music.

Roger throws his feet apart and starts dancing like a monkey, bopping up and down, and picking imaginary bananas. A bunch of other kids stream onto the dance floor and imitate his moves.

The audience clap their hands to the crazy beat, laughing at all the goofy dancers.

Roger grabs Charlene and swings her around. When he puts her down, she ends up with her feet on the star. But Roger is no longer on the star.

Suddenly the disco ball lowers from the ceiling, and a bright-pink laser beam shoots out and zaps Charlene. She instantly vanishes. In her place a small pile of bright-pink powder sits in the middle of the star, courtesy of Dominic's special effects.

The music stops. The dancers freeze.

"What happened?" asks Roger. "Where'd she go? I don't understand. Why'd the music stop?"

Drew enters, dressed in blue overalls and carrying a whisk broom and a small dustpan. Without saying a word, he quickly sweeps up the pile of bright-pink powder and exits.

"You took your feet off the star, Roger. You can't do that. You can dance all you want, but you have to keep your feet on the star." I position Roger back on top of the star. "Okay, Roger?"

"I love to dance!"

"Fantastic. Just remember what I said. All right, start the music!" I press a button on the remote control.

Sophie plays the flügelhorn as the Astro-Nuts Band clangs kettle gongs and thumps drums.

Roger places his left hand on his hip and throws his right hand in the air, pointing his index finger toward the ceiling. He wiggles his hips back and forth. The other dancers imitate his every move while the audience claps along.

Suddenly Roger grabs Audrey and twirls her

around. Just like before, she ends up dancing on the star in his place.

Once again the laser beam shoots from the disco ball and Audrey vanishes. Again a small pile of powder sits in the middle of the star. Everything stops.

"What's going on?" asks Roger. "No dance? Why no dance?"

Farley reenters and sweeps up the new pile of bright-pink powder.

"Roger, once again you took your feet off the star. How many times do I have to tell you? If you want to dance—"

"I love to dance!"

"Then you have to keep your feet on the star." I move Roger back on top of the star.

"No, Mr. Truth Police," says Roger. "*You* keep *your* feet on it!" He pulls me onto the star and deliberately steps off it with a grin.

The disco ball fires a pink laser beam. I vanish. Another small pile of bright-pink powder sits in my place.

Roger stares at the pink powder, then looks to the

camera, starry eyed. "I love to dance!" he exclaims, raising a clenched fist in the air.

The music blasts again. Roger dances wildly all over the dance floor, like a total lunatic.

The audience inside the Black Box cheers and woo-hoos. The throngs of kids watching the show on the TruthScreen in the mess hall roar with glee. The hundreds of kids watching in the amphitheater stomp their feet and chant. "*Astro-Nuts! Astro-Nuts!* We're nutty for *Astro-Nuts!*"

It's awesome. *Astro-Nuts* is a colossal hit!

Chapter 50

Sophie and the Astro-Nuts Band bang away at their instruments.

Boing! Clonk! Bwraap!

Everyone walks over to center stage, and we all grin goofily at one another. I haven't felt this happy since . . . ever.

The entire cast take our final bows. We put our arms around one another's shoulders and then swing and sway.

Large Marge and Bucky Buckner join us onstage. Swayzee picks up his eleven-stringed Wazooper and belts out another verse of the Astro-Nuts song.

WE'RE NUTTY, NUTTY ASTRO-NUTS!
E'RE SO SORRY BUT THIS ENDS OUR SHOW!
WE'RE NUTTY, NUTTY ASTRO-NUTS!
GOOD-BYE TILL THE NEXT TIME WE SAY HELLO!

Even Sergeant Sergeant gets into the act. He slips in between Drew and Charlene. He throws his arms around their shoulders.

Drew looks uneasy. Charlene seems a bit creeped out. But they continue swinging and swaying.

In the control room, Dominic rolls the credits.

Large Marge thrusts her fists in the air. "And that's a wrap!"

Sergeant Sergeant turns to Charlene. He purses his lips to give her a peck on the cheek.

"Let's not ruin the moment," Charlene tells him.

She throws both of her arms around me and gives me a huge hug. I return the favor.

Sergeant Sergeant sulks away.

Charlene looks into my eyes. "I'm so proud of you," she says. "You were really funny. Totally hysterical."

Then she leans in and kisses me. On the lips.

Fireworks go off in my brain.

It's my first kiss. Ever.

We hold each other's hands and gaze into each other's eyes. The Black Box is jam-packed with loud people, but Charlene and I are alone in a world of our own.

She smiles from ear to ear. So do I. Right back at her. Then I get sad.

"What's wrong?" she asks. She sees it in my eyes.

"I just wish my parents could have seen me tonight."

Dominic pokes my shoulder. "Maybe they did," he says as Drew and Sophie gather round.

"Did you find my parents? Did you get into my permanent record?"

"Not exactly," says Dominic.

"What do you mean?"

"I downloaded everything from Sergeant Sergeant's Truthcorder, but...I didn't see anyone's permanent records. Maybe we were wrong about them being in there. Sorry, Norbert."

"How is that even possible? They *have* to be there!"

"You promised you wouldn't get mad."

"I'm not mad. I'm upset. There's a difference. Now what do we d—"

"I never had anyone's permanent records on my Truthcorder." Sergeant Sergeant walks over and stares me down.

He's been eavesdropping the entire time. Figures.

He taps the device. "I use this thing to design and play video games."

"Seriously?" asks Dominic.

"Do you really expect us to believe that?" asks Drew.

I look Sergeant Sergeant straight in the eyes. "If you don't have our permanent records, how do you know where my parents are?"

"I have no idea where your parents are."

"But we distinctly heard you," says Sophie. "You said, 'I know exactly where they're hidden, and no one will ever figure it out.'"

"I was talking about the hidden characters in the Astro-Nuts video game I'm designing," says Sergeant Sergeant. He shows us the screen. Little blue aliens zigzag through a 3-D maze as hot-pink spiders bounce around and yellow spaceships float helter-skelter. "I'm on Level Five."

I can hardly believe it. "Then why have you been spying on me ever since I got here?"

"I haven't been spying on you," says Sergeant

Sergeant. "I've been looking out for you. Who do you think recommended you for this television show in the first place?"

Whoa. Suddenly all of Sergeant Sergeant's strange behavior makes perfect sense. Well, most of it. He's still a pretty quirky guy.

"I'm sorry," I tell him. "I guess I really had you pegged all wrong."

"No problem, Norbert Riddle, Nonperson Number L4LUZR-1. You're not the first person to misjudge me." He glances at Charlene, Dominic, Drew, and Sophie.

"But how will I ever find my parents now?" I ask. There's a pause.

Then Charlene speaks up "Dominic, you said Norbert's parents may have seen the show. What did you mean by that?"

Dominic's eye twitches. "I don't know how I did it, but by hacking into the mainframe computer, I accidentally broadcast the whole *Astro-Nuts* show out into space. Everywhere. Across the entire universe."

"Including Earth?" I goggle at him.

Dominic nods. "The show got sent to every single TruthScreen on Earth."

My mouth nearly hits the floor. "That means Loving Leader and the Truth Police saw everything."

"I'm afraid so," says Dominic. "But maybe your parents saw it too and now they know where you are."

"Yeah, but Loving Leader and the Truth Police also know exactly where we are."

Drew shakes his head. "We're doomed," he says.

"Most definitely," adds Sophie.

"Barren asteroid, here we come," says Charlene.

My heart sinks. "I'm never going to see my parents again, am I?"

"That's the least of your worries," says Sergeant Sergeant. "Besides, your parents are probably dead anyway."

Tears well up in my eyes. I swallow hard. I feel like Sergeant Sergeant just punched me in the gut.

Charlene turns to Sergeant Sergeant. "How can you be so cruel?" she asks.

"Me?" asks Sergeant Sergeant. "He's the one who

got us all into this stupid mess. And now we're all dead too."

Charlene puts her arm around my shoulders. Sophie gives the two of us a big hug.

But here's the thing. Deep down I suspect Sergeant Sergeant is right.

Dead right.

Chapter 51

The next thing I know, I'm sitting in the old comfy chair again. The one in front of Bucky's big glass desk.

I'm not alone. I'm surrounded by the entire cast of *Astro-Nuts*. We're all in a serious jam. And I'm not talking blueberry.

It's an emergency meeting. Bucky paces back and forth behind his desk. "People," he says, "we've got a problem. A big problem."

"Ginormous," says Drew.

"That's putting it mildly," says Charlene.

I'm racked with guilt. If I hadn't been so obsessed with finding my parents, we wouldn't be in this horrible predicament in the first place. My whole body shivers. I feel like I'm plummeting from the sky aboard one of Dominic's helicycles. Only, this time I'm definitely going to crash into Danger Desert and get sucked into the high-speed quicksand by huge, slimy tentacles.

"We've got to come up with a reasonable explanation," says Bucky. He takes a seat in his chair.

"There is no reasonable explanation," says Large Marge.

"How about an unreasonable explanation?" asks Drew.

A mechanical clank diverts our attention. We all look to the ceiling.

A long, narrow metal flap tosses open, revealing a slender slot. The large TruthScreen lowers from the opening. Whirring. Slowly. Until it covers the entire wall behind Bucky's desk.

Bucky swivels around in his chair to face the screen. He folds his hands on his lap.

The TruthScreen lights up.

We all gasp. In unison. Not intentionally. Automatically.

Penetrating eyes scrutinize us. They're fierce. Intense. Threatening.

A furious face confronts us. The vicious face of a man with wild white hair.

He wears a gray jumpsuit. His right hand reaches out from the screen and points at each one of us.

LOVING LEADER SHARES THE LOVE.

"So you *dare* to call yourselves Astro-Nuts!" says Loving Leader in a booming voice. "Why, you're nothing but Astro-*Naughties*! How dare you defy my authority! How dare you mock His All-Knowing Eternal Excellency!"

He looks like his head is going to explode or something. I hope it does.

I'm fed up with this big bully. I mean, seriously, can't the guy take a joke? I don't mind when people poke fun at me; I can laugh at myself. After all, nobody's perfect, but I guess Loving Leader thinks he is. He probably hasn't looked in a mirror recently. He really should. He'd crack up laughing.

And what kind of person can't shrug it off? Someone who takes himself way too seriously, that's who. Someone who wants to control the way everyone lives. Someone threatened by anyone with a spark of imagination. I used to think Loving Leader really did love us. But Loving Leader loves just one thing. Himself.

I rise from the chair.

Everyone in Bucky's office looks at me like I've completely lost my mind. Charlene shakes her head at me, hoping I get the message and sit back down.

I point my finger right back at Loving Leader. "You know, you really need to lighten up."

Everyone gasps, including Loving Leader.

"How dare you criticize His All-Knowing Eternal Excellency!" he shouts.

"You're not all-knowing. You don't even know yourself! You're just a control freak trying to control everything and everyone. We're not out of control. *You* are."

"Control freak, am I? Loving Leader is no control freak! Loving Leader just knows what's best for everyone else!"

"Instead of trying to control everyone else, you need to control yourself."

"Silence, Norbert Riddle, Nonperson Number L4LUZR-1! No one cares what you think! Sit back down before I make mincemeat out of you!"

I retreat to the comfy chair and zip my mouth shut.

"There are limits to freedom of expression!" yells Loving Leader. "Because there *is* no freedom of expression! Just limits!"

Loving Leader orders Bucky to cease all production on *Astro-Nuts*, seal off the Black Box, and round up everyone responsible—immediately! Without further ado. Whatever that is.

His All-Knowing Eternal Excellency points to each one of us. "It is illegal under section 6,787,382, paragraph 4,653, of the criminal code to insult Loving Leader or the government of the United State of Earth. Criminal proceedings will commence immediately against everyone involved in the production of the *Astro-Nuts* show. Especially you, Norbert Riddle, Nonperson Number L4LUZR-1. When found guilty, as you all surely will be, offenders will face a life sentence of breaking boulders with a sledgehammer on a barren asteroid."

We're all stunned into silence.

Then Drew leans over and whispers in my ear. "Well, look on the bright side. Maybe that's where your parents are."

Chapter 52

But wait.

On the TruthScreen someone hands a sheet of paper to Loving Leader. We can't see exactly who. All we see is an arm.

Loving Leader takes the sheet of paper. The arm pulls back off the screen in a split second. I get the funny feeling the messenger ran away as quickly as possible to avoid being blamed for more bad news.

His All-Knowing Eternal Excellency reads the notice to himself. His eyes dart back and forth. He sneers. Not a good sign.

Loving Leader doesn't look happy. He crumples

up the memo and tosses it aside. He squints his eyes and glares directly at me.

"I've just been handed an urgent bulletin," he says.

Duh.

Based on the way Loving Leader scowls at me, I'm guessing our punishment is about to get much worse than breaking boulders with a sledgehammer on a barren asteroid for the rest of our lives.

I know Drew creamed up the whole Powder Room idea. But if Loving Leader saw that sketch on *Astro-Nuts*, I'm pretty sure he plans to build a real-life Powder Room to zap us all into bright-pink powder that he'll sweep up into test tubes, label with our serial numbers and place in storage—forever. Possibly longer.

"This changes everything." Loving Leader makes a fist with his right hand and punches the palm of his left hand. "It seems every single solitary person on Earth saw *Astro-Nuts* tonight. All sixty-seven billion citizens of the United State of Earth."

Bucky Buckner gulps so hard the sound can be heard clear across the Orion Nebula.

"And how do you think they're reacting?" Loving Leader holds up a remote control. "Take a look!"

The picture switches to a sweeping view of oppressive gray skyscrapers, gray skies, gray everything.

The camera zooms in. Massive crowds occupy the streets. Hundreds of thousands of people, all wearing gray jumpsuits. They're cheering, chanting, and carrying banners. It's a massive Love Fest. Bigger than any Love Fest I've ever seen.

I can't make out what the people are chanting. The camera moves in closer.

People hold up a banner that reads: LONG LIVE LOVING LEADER!

Another banner says: LONG LIVE *ASTRO-NUTS*!

Huh?

I suddenly make out what the crowd is chanting.

"*Astro-Nuts*!" they shout. "We love *Astro-Nuts*! We love Loving Leader! Long live Loving Leader! Long live *Astro-Nuts*!"

The picture on the TruthScreen switches to another gray city. More tall gray buildings, same old gray skies. And another whopping Love Fest. What are the people chanting? "*Astro-Nuts* forever! *Astro-Nuts* forever!*"

A homemade sign says: I LOVE TO DANCE!

A huge banner reads: WE'RE NUTTY FOR *ASTRO-NUTS*!

The picture on the TruthScreen switches from city to city. All around Earth, citizens are cheering for Loving Leader! *Astro-Nuts* is a monster hit.

And here's the kicker.

They think Loving Leader is a terrific sport for letting us make fun of him.

They're convinced Loving Leader is even more loving than ever before.

Ain't that a kick in the pants?

Chapter 53

Loving Leader's face appears again on the Truth-Screen. He starts congratulating us and telling us how funny we are. We're no longer enemies of the state. Suddenly we're national heroes! He wants us to keep on producing *Astro-Nuts* and broadcasting the show to the entire universe—but especially Earth.

"But Loving Leader," says Bucky, "how can we produce the show if we're serving life sentences breaking boulders with a sledgehammer on a barren asteroid?"

"You didn't take me seriously, did you? I was just joking. I *want* you to make fun of me. In fact, I *order* you to make fun of me!"

So everything goes back to normal at Astro-Nuts Camp.

I mean abnormal.

We start planning for the next *Astro-Nuts* show, with Loving Leader's blessing. But one question still haunts me. Where are my parents? And how will I ever find them? Okay, I admit that's really two questions.

A week goes by. Drew, Sophie, and I are sitting in the meadow, thinking up ideas for the next show. I'm no longer wearing a gray jumpsuit. It's now neon green. I finally let Farley Chung help me pick out new clothes that express my personality. And stand out in a crowd.

All of a sudden we hear a distant roar.

A sleek silver spaceship descends from the sky. A set of spidery legs opens. The ship touches down on the far side of the meadow, in the exact same spot where it landed last time. Well, maybe three inches to the left.

The door to the spaceship springs open. Icy smoke whooshes out.

A gruff man wearing a tight-fitting space suit and a Viking helmet emerges from the cloud of smoke. As he climbs down the ladder, I spot his scraggly black hair and a trimmed black beard.

"It's Grissom," says Drew. "He's back."

"But why so soon?" asks Sophie.

Yeah, he's not supposed to return for at least

another five months. Something's up. Something weird.

Two silhouettes appear in the open doorway. Is Grissom delivering new inmates? Who are they?

The icy smoke clears.

A man in a gray jumpsuit. A woman in a gray jumpsuit.

Could it be?

NEW ARRIVALS?

Did Grissom bring my parents to Zorquat 3? I run toward the spaceship. Drew and Sophie chase after me.

Before I reach the man and woman, Grissom catches me in his arms. He lifts me up and looks me straight in the eyes. Grissom is a big guy. He could crush me like a grapefruit. Or a golf ball. Your choice.

"You kill me," says Grissom.

Uh-oh.

His eyes twinkle. "I almost busted a gut," he says. "You're a hoot, Norbert. I love *Astro-Nuts*! Funniest show ever!"

I start breathing again. "Thank you," I say.

"I brought you a surprise." He lowers me back down to the ground.

Three golden robot guards emerge from the spaceship and lower themselves down the ladder. One after the other. They beep and buzz.

Then Grissom brandishes his hand, directing my attention to the man and woman in gray jumpsuits climbing down the ladder from the spaceship.

My jaw drops to my toes. I'm in total shock. Completely speechless.

"Norbert! Norbert! You didn't forget all about us, did you?"

"Aunt Martha? Uncle Hank?"

"Oh, Norbert!" says Aunt Martha. "I'm so happy to see you."

"Me too!" says Uncle Hank. "We've been so worried about you."

"But I don't understand. What are you two doing here? Did the Truth Police arrest you? Is all this my fault? I'm so sorry. I never meant to get you two in trouble. Will you ever forgive me?"

Aunt Martha shakes her head. "No, Norbert. It's nothing like that."

The robots stand poised in the meadow, holding their laser guns. Their heads swivel and whir. The menacing red lights in their eye sockets flash.

"Loving Leader sent us," says Uncle Hank.

"Did he give you both a life sentence?"

"You don't understand," says Aunt Martha. "He sent us here to bring you back home."

I can't believe my ears. I look to Grissom.

"Is this some sort of trick?"

"It's all true," he says. "Truly, truthfully true. We're here to bring you and the entire cast and crew of *Astro-Nuts* back to Earth. You'll all be hailed as heroes and given your own state-of-the-art television studio to produce your show. And *Astro-Nuts* will be officially broadcast on the one and only official TruthScreen channel!"

I don't know what to say. I'm completely flabbergasted. Ever since I got here, all I've wanted to do is go home to find my parents, but I never expected this would happen in a million years. No, make that a billion years.

I should be jumping for joy, pumping my fists in the air, and hugging Grissom, Aunt Martha, and Uncle Hank like crazy. But for some strange reason, I'm just standing here in a daze—totally confused. I've got the awful feeling there's something wrong here, but I just can't put my finger on it.

I mean, you'd think I'd be on cloud nine now that my prayers have been answered.

But have they?

Then it hits me. If Loving Leader really wants

me to return to Earth, why did he send Aunt Martha and Uncle Hank to get me? Why not my mother and father?

I turn to my aunt and uncle. "My parents," I mutter. "Are they still…alive?"

Aunt Martha looks to Uncle Hank. He bites his lower lip, stares at the ground, and shakes his head. This can't be good.

Aunt Martha looks into my eyes. She's crying.

"We don't know," she whimpers. "We'll probably never know."

Then she does something she's never done before. She gives me a huge hug.

That's when I start bawling. I may never stop.

Chapter 54

That night banging drums muster everyone to another Love Fest in the amphitheater. Hundreds of kids pack into the tiers of benches.

Crazy Swayzee circles around the teetering wood tower in the center of the pit, pouring zapolyne rocket fuel all over the bottom legs. The wobbly tower rises higher than ever before. It looks a lot shakier, too.

Drew and I sit alongside tonight's special guests. Aunt Martha and Uncle Hank seem even shakier than the tower of firewood. They've attended Love Fests back on Earth, but they've never seen anything like *this*. They're incredibly leery, especially when

Swayzee pours a spiraling trail of zapolyne around the tower, and the crowd starts clapping their hands and stomping their feet.

Aunt Martha and Uncle Hank shiver with fear when the kids chant, "Insanity! Insanity! Gives you personality!"

Drew turns to my aunt and uncle. "So, Aunt Martha, what did you and Uncle Hank think of our show?"

Aunt Martha hesitates. She looks to Uncle Hank. My uncle shrugs and scratches the back of his head.

Aunt Martha turns to Drew. "Well, kids, I have to confess. I really didn't understand most of it. I know it's supposed to be funny. But I just don't get it."

"Norbert does a great impersonation of Loving Leader." Uncle Hank pats my head. "You could take his place and no one would know the difference."

Charlene Gordon joins us just in the nick of time. She wears her long blond hair in a bun, held in place with a pair of chopsticks again. I introduce her to my aunt and uncle.

"She seems like a very nice girl," Aunt Martha whispers in my ear. "But what are those sticks in her hair?"

"Antennae," I say, pointing to the chopsticks.

Charlene giggles.

Sophie starts playing the keyboard, and the other musicians bang, clunk, whump, and thump their weird assortment of instruments.

Everyone rises to their feet, lifts their right hand in the air, and holds up one finger to make the letter *I*. They start jumping up and down, chanting, "Imagination! Imagination! Everyone join our celebration!"

Aunt Martha nearly faints. Uncle Hank steadies her.

Down in the pit, Swayzee lights the end of the zapolyne trail on the ground. As a bright orange flame races around the wobbling tower, Howie Rubenstein chases after it with his camera, snapping photos.

Ka-boom! Boom! Boom!

The bonfire explodes in a magnificent blaze. Everyone bursts into cheers.

Swayzee steps up to a microphone, howls at the two moons, and starts strumming his Wazooper. After leading a brief sing-along, he introduces our warden, "The one and only Bucky Buckner!"

Everyone applauds like crazy. "Bucky! Bucky! Bucky!" we chant.

Sergeant Sergeant sits nearby. He stops tapping his Truthcorder and pumps his fist in the air. I'm guessing he just completed Level 6.

When we all settle down, Bucky takes the microphone.

"My fellow Astro-Nuts! I'm delighted and overjoyed to report that our top secret project—our *Astro-Nuts* show—is a bigger success than we ever imagined possible. And that's saying a lot, considering we all have pretty big imaginations. But no one ever imagined that Loving Leader would love *Astro-Nuts* and ask us to bring the entire cast and crew back to Earth to produce the show for TruthScreens everywhere! And so, tonight I'd like to introduce our special guest. The Astro-Nut who brought all of you here and delivered the equipment to make the show. An Astro-Nut who needs no introduction…your friend and mine, Grissom!"

We all cheer.

Grissom steps up to the microphone. He carries a

large gold trophy that looks like a statue of Loving Leader. Everyone quiets down.

"Thank you, Bucky. Tonight I'd like to present the Loving Leader Award to all the Astro-Nuts who helped make our *Astro-Nuts* show such a huge hit. Everyone in the cast and crew, come on down!"

The crowd explodes with applause. The band breaks into song, banging kettle gongs and crashing cymbals.

Sophie rises from behind her keyboard and steps up to the stage. Drew, Charlene, Roger, Farley, and Dominic join her, along with everyone else involved with the show. Yeah, me too.

"Which one of you would like to accept this award on behalf of the entire group?"

Roger looks like he's ready to grab the trophy. Instead he points to...me. "Norbert!" he yells.

"Norbert!" shouts Sophie with all her heart.

"Norbert!" chimes in Drew, pumping his fist in the air.

"Norbert!" cheers Charlene, a sparkle in her eye.

Suddenly they're all chanting, "Norbert! Norbert! Norbert!" Even Sergeant Sergeant.

It's incredible. I can almost feel my parents smiling down on me.

"Looks like it's unanimous," announces Grissom. "So here he is to accept the Loving Leader Award for the cast and crew of *Astro-Nuts*, the Astro-Nut you know and love for his dazzling wit and impressive impressions—Norbert Riddle!"

The audience erupts into applause.

My friends push me forward. Grissom gives me a high five and hands me the gold statue of Loving Leader. I raise the statue in the air.

The crowd goes insane. I approach the microphone.

Everyone quiets down.

I take a deep breath. "Since the moment I got here, I've wanted to go home. I hated it here right from the start. But the truth is...this is the nicest place I've ever been. And you're the nicest people I've ever met. It took me a while to figure that out. But from day one you've encouraged and nurtured my creativity. You've pushed me to be even funnier.

You've helped me realize that, yes, I am different. Yes, I am dangerous. And now, thanks to all of you, I'm proud of who and what I really am."

The crowd hoots, whistles, and woo-hoos.

"But now I've got a big announcement to make. Drew, Sophie, all of us—we've discussed it among ourselves, and we've come to a unanimous decision."

I look to Charlene. She bites her lower lip.

"We've decided we don't want to be rescued. We never want to go back to Earth. We want to stay right here on Zorquat Three, where people truly appreciate our talents."

Thunderous applause. Large Marge raises her fists in the air. Charlene's wide smile warms my heart.

Aunt Martha and Uncle Hank look completely stunned.

"And one more thing," I say. "We don't need no stinkin' trophies!"

I hurl my statue of Loving Leader into the bonfire.

The Astro-Nuts go completely nuts.

This time Aunt Martha really does faint. Right into Uncle Hank's arms.

Chapter 55

"Now, Norbert, are you absolutely certain you want to stay here?" asks Aunt Martha.

"This place is definitely a certifiable madhouse," says Uncle Hank. "I've never had hot dogs and hamburgers for breakfast before in my life!"

We're strolling together across the meadow, walking toward the spaceship. It's the morning after the Love Fest. Someday morning, the eighth day of the week.

"Yeah, I'm positive," I say. "I love hot dogs and hamburgers for breakfast. That's why I love it here.

It's crazy town twenty-one hours a day, eight days a week."

I don't tell Aunt Martha and Uncle Hank that there's no way I'll ever go back to live in their dreary gray house on a dreary gray planet if my parents are gone forever. Saying that would just hurt my aunt and uncle's feelings. After all, if they're happy taking inventory in a thumbtack warehouse and watching a machine insert cotton into aspirin bottles for the rest of their lives, who am I to rain on their parade?

The three robots remain poised with their laser guns, guarding the spaceship. Their heads swivel and whir. Their beady red-light eyes flicker.

Over by the flagpole, Grissom speaks privately with Crazy Swayzee. They're whispering. It's all very mysterious. They look in my direction, nodding knowingly.

They're talking about me. I just know it. I wonder what they're saying. What if they're planning to drag me aboard the ship? I tell myself to stop what-iffing.

"Well, I'll be!" shouts Swayzee. He looks up to the sky and lets out a long howl.

Aunt Martha turns to me. "Are you really sure about this?"

I smile and nod. I hug my aunt. My uncle, too.

"Ready, folks?" Grissom pats my aunt and uncle on the back.

Swayzee remains at the flagpole. He stands with

his thumbs stuck in his pockets, whistling the *Astro-Nuts* theme song. Just waiting for the spaceship to take off.

"So long, Norbert," says Aunt Martha. Tears run down her cheeks.

"Take good care of yourself," says Uncle Hank. He wipes a tear from his eye.

"Make 'em laugh," says Grissom. He gives me a big thumbs-up.

As Aunt Martha and Uncle Hank climb up the spaceship ladder, Large Marge comes running out of the woods. She throws her arms around Grissom and hugs him. Tight. She gives him a big kiss. Their Viking helmets clank. "Now, you be sure to write, you big lummox," she says.

"Will do." Grissom straightens his Viking helmet and shoots up the ladder to the spaceship. One at a time, the robot guards follow after him. The door to the spaceship whisks shut and clanks tight.

Large Marge and I saunter backward across the meadow and join Swayzee at the flagpole. The three of us wave good-bye to the spaceship.

I'm sad to see Aunt Martha and Uncle Hank go, but even they know this is where I belong.

With a rumble the rocket lifts off and soars into the bright blue sky.

I see Sergeant Sergeant standing in his watchtower, tracking the spaceship through his high-powered binoculars.

We all shout and wave good-bye to the spaceship, except for Sergeant Sergeant, who yells, "Good riddance!"

And then—*blamo!*—Grissom's ship vanishes into space.

I turn to Swayzee. "So what was all that about?"

"What was all *what* about?"

"You and Grissom. What's so hush-hush?"

"Oh, that."

Large Marge raises her eyebrows. Her ears prick up too.

"It's confidential," says Swayzee. "Top secret."

"I can take a hint." Large Marge throws up her hands. "I know where I'm not wanted." She heads back to Girls Unit 3.

Swayzee starts whistling the *Astro-Nuts* theme

song again—until Large Marge disappears across the meadow. Then he turns to me. He raises his hand to cover his mouth. "Someone wants to see you," he whispers. "Someone who saw you on *Astro-Nuts*. Someone even more important than Loving Leader."

I'm dumbstruck. Who could that higher power be? Someone worse than Loving Leader? Am I now in some sort of big trouble for refusing to go back to Earth with Aunt Martha and Uncle Hank?

"We better get you out of here," says Swayzee.

Something tells me I may have just made the biggest mistake of my life.

Chapter 56

"Let's just make sure Sergeant Sergeant doesn't see us," whispers Swayzee.

Swayzee heads for the trees. He hides behind one tree and then scoots over to another. I follow his every move.

When we get far enough away from the watchtower, we stop hopping from tree to tree. Now we hike like normal people through the woods. Not that either one of us is normal.

"Where are we going?" I ask.

"Somewhere safe," says Swayzee.

We reach a huge, sunny green pasture filled with

gonzosauruses—striped, polka-dot, argyle, paisley—grazing in the grass.

"How come you don't keep them penned up in a corral?" I ask.

"No need. They graze right here. Happy in the wild. Tame. And super friendly. Besides, no corral we build is ever going to hold a gonzosaurus."

Swayzee walks over to Princess, the purple gonzosaurus with large pink spots. "Hey, girl," he says.

Princess lowers her head and scoops up Swayzee. He slides down her long neck and into the saddle on her back.

Then, picking me up with her mouth, she places me behind Swayzee.

I wrap my arms around his waist.

"Hold on tight, buckaroo." Swayzee straightens the cowboy hat on his head. "Giddyup!" he shouts.

Princess tromps across the pasture, slogs along the banks of a babbling brook, and traipses into the woods.

We traverse a familiar swamp. We trek through the forest. In the lush valley I spot Dominic Garcia's outdoor workshop.

Princess lowers her head, and Swayzee and I slide down her long neck to the ground.

Swayzee grabs two plastic helmets and tosses one to me. I strap it on my head. Swayzee wears his helmet over his cowboy hat. It's an interesting look.

We hop aboard individual helicycles and start pedaling. The narrow blades whirl and we rise into the air, hovering high in the sky.

We see Astro-Nuts Camp in the distance. I wonder if I'll ever see it again. We fly over the tall mountaintop. From the peak the waterfall cascades into the beautiful lake below.

Then Swayzee waves his hand and points toward Danger Desert.

Is he nuts? Has he completely lost his marbles?

If we crash into Danger Desert, that high-speed quicksand—or something worse—will suck us under in the blink of an eye.

But Swayzee turns the handlebars of his helicycle and starts to fly over the vast sands.

I take a deep breath and follow after him.

We pedal like maniacs. Faster than I've ever

pedaled anything in my life. Neither one of us wants to tumble into those hungry sands directly beneath us. No sirree Bob. Who's Bob? I have no idea.

I just know one thing. I can't look down.

We head for the hundreds of huge eggs on the green horizon. We're past Danger Desert now. Rolling green hills stretch out beneath us. Eggs of all different beautiful colors and patterns lie scattered in the greenery.

As we pedal closer, I notice something strange. The eggs have windows and doors. They're not eggs at all. They're houses and buildings shaped like eggs and painted with designs that match the patterns of gonzosauruses.

We gently land our helicycles in a grassy meadow and lay them down in the wildflowers.

"What is this place?" I ask.

"Eccentric City." Swayzee removes his plastic helmet and straightens his cowboy hat on his head. "This is as far as I go, partner." He points to an egg-shaped house painted with beautiful swirls of green.

"Go ahead," he says.

"Go ahead and what?" I ask.

"Knock."

Chapter 57

"**A**ren't you coming with me?"

"I'll be perfectly fine right here." Swayzee ducks behind a tree.

"But who's in there?" I ask.

Swayzee pokes his head around the trunk. "There's only one way to find out "

"Well, you could just tell me."

"Sorry, I can't The person inside wants to see you, Norbert. Not little ole me." He ducks his head again. He's not called Crazy Swayzee for nothing.

I'm not sure what to do. What if I knock at the door, and the Truth Police swarm out and wrestle me to the ground? There I go again. What if this? What if that? What if nothing?

I move slowly toward the door. One step at a time.

I look back at the tree.

Swayzee's head peeps out again. With a flick of his wrist, he gestures for me to go ahead and knock at the door.

I get up my nerve and rap my knuckles on the door three times.

I wait.

Nothing. Maybe I should just run back and hide behind that tree with Swayzee while I've still got a chance.

The door squeaks open. Just a crack.

It's dark inside. Completely black. All I can see are a pair of eyes. They stare at me intently.

"Hello," I say. "I'm Norbert Riddle. You asked to see me?"

The door opens a bit more. Then swings wide open. A lady stands before me. She seems surprised to see me.

"Norbert!" she exclaims. "Is that really you?"

"Were you expecting someone else?"

"Don't you recognize me?"

I study her for a moment. Her straight, black hair, caring eyes, and sweet smile look familiar, but I can't place the face. I shake my head no.

"It's me," she says.

Everything suddenly registers.

"Mom?" My mouth drops open.

My mother opens her arms and I leap into them.

Tears of joy. Sobs. Waterworks. The whole kit and caboodle.

"Oh, Norbert, I can't believe it's really you."

"I thought you and Dad were dead," I say. "Or turned into pink powder!"

"I've missed you something awful," she says.

"Not as much as I've missed you!"

She invites me inside. Swayzee, too. She caught a glimpse of his head sticking out from behind the tree.

"Howdy, ma'am. The name's Tex," he says. "Tex Swayzee. I'm Norbert's counselor."

"Thank you for bringing my son to me." My mother shakes his hand. "I'm Yoshiko Riddle. It's a pleasure to meet you. Please, come inside. You two must be starving."

Her house is filled with her paintings—canvases covered with wild splatters of color.

She pours us tall glasses of lemonade and makes soup and sandwiches. It's a regular banquet.

We talk. And talk. And talk.

She tells us that after the Truth Police arrested her, the judge at her Truth Trial sentenced her to a prison for adults on Zorquat 3. And now here she is.

I tell her everything that happened to me, and Mom explains how she found me. She shows me the TruthScreen in her living room.

I flinch. "Can Loving Leader see us?"

"No, Norbert," she says. "Our TruthScreens only receive shows broadcast on Zorquat Three, like *Astro-Nuts*. I recognized you immediately. I relayed a secret message to Grissom, and, well, here you are. You were terrific on that show, by the way. I'm so proud of you. You're just like your father."

"Where is he?"

Her face saddens. She looks to her feet. "You don't want to know."

"Yes, I do."

"Trust me, you really don't."

"Mom, I'm not a little kid anymore."

She looks me up and down. A smile plays on her lips. "You're right," she says. "Follow me."

My mother brings me outside to the backyard. She points her finger up at the sky. "Your father's up there."

I look up to see what she's pointing at.

It's the purple moon.

I don't understand. "What's he doing up there?"

"He's a prisoner in a horrible labor camp, working in an underground mine."

Tears fill my eyes.

"Well," I say. "I guess we'll just have to figure out a way to go up there and get him."

My mother hugs me. Super tight.

Like she's never going to let go. Ever.

Epilogue

And that's my story.

Well, so far.

You've probably got a whole slew of questions. So let me tie up some of the loose ends for you.

My mother invites me to live with her in her fancy egg-shaped house. "You're more than welcome here, Norbert. But I have to warn you. Only grownups live in Eccentric City. It's like Astro-Nuts Camp for adults. You'll be the only kid in town."

I definitely want to say yes, but to tell you the truth, I'm really torn. If I move in with my mother,

I'll miss all the great new friends I've made back at Astro-Nuts Camp.

Tough decision.

"So what do you say, Norbert?"

"I'd love to stay, Mom, but they really need me back at Astro-Nuts Camp. I'm running our next *Astro-Nuts* show. And the next show. And the show after that. Everyone's depending on me."

"Then that's where you belong," she says.

But there's no way I can just leave her here after finally finding her. "Mom, why don't you come live at Astro-Nuts Camp?"

"I don't know about that, Norbert. What would I do there?"

"You could teach art. There's a whole studio with kids who love to throw paint."

She rubs her chin. "Let me sleep on it."

Swayzee and I stay overnight at my mom's house. That night she tucks me into bed. She kisses my forehead and sings me a lullaby: "Twinkle, Twinkle, Little Star." What are the odds of that?

The next morning during breakfast, my mother gives us her answer.

Swayzee and I ride our helicycles back across Danger Desert to the top of the tall mountain peak.

And my mother? She's right behind me, with her arms wrapped around my waist.

We fold up our helicycles and zip down the wire to the flagpole at Astro-Nuts Camp.

Everyone welcomes us with cheers! I introduce Mom to all my friends. Bucky assigns her to a private cabin and puts her in charge of the paint balloon room. I'm thrilled and grateful to have her back in my life.

I immediately get to work on the next *Astro-Nuts* show.

I've never been happier in my life. Well, that's not the truly true truth. There's still one thing missing.

My dad.

I think of him every time I look up at the purple moon.

So does my mother. It breaks her heart. Mine too. He's so close, yet so far away.

When do I plan to rescue him?

Someday.

Yep, Someday soon.

I'm sure it won't be long before I come up with a surefire, foolproof plan. Something different. And definitely dangerous.

I can't tell you exactly what I'm going to do, because it's pretty hard to predict the future. Unless you have a time machine. Fortunately, Dominic Garcia just started building one.

Who knows? Maybe I'll use Dominic's time machine to rescue my father. After all, the only limit is my imagination.

Then again, I have no idea if Dominic will ever get his time machine to actually work. I just hope he gets all the bugs out before he tests it. I don't know about you, but the last thing I want to do is travel through time with a whole bunch of bugs.

I'm obviously going to need a little help from my friends. I'm sure I can count on Drew And I just know Sophie will pitch in. Charlene, too. Right now they're sitting together at the keyboard and playing the classic song "Chopsticks." Of course, things could change at the drop of a hat. So I'm keeping a close eye to make sure no one drops any hats.

In the meantime, I have to get back to the Black Box.

I've got a show to do.

Imagine that!

About the Authors

JAMES PATTERSON received the Literarian Award for Outstanding Service to the American Literary Community from the National Book Foundation. He holds the Guinness World Record for the most #1 *New York Times* bestsellers, including *Middle School, I Funny,* and *Jacky Ha-Ha,* and his books have sold more than 375 million copies worldwide. A tireless champion of the power of books and reading, Patterson created a children's book imprint, JIMMY Patterson, whose mission is simple: "We want every kid who finishes a JIMMY Book to say, 'PLEASE GIVE ME ANOTHER BOOK.'" He has donated more than one million books to students and soldiers and funds over four hundred Teacher Education Scholarships at twenty-four colleges and universities. He has also donated millions of dollars to independent bookstores and school libraries. Patterson invests proceeds from the sales of JIMMY Patterson Books in pro-reading initiatives.

JOEY GREEN, a former contributing editor to *National Lampoon,* is the author of more than sixty books. He has appeared on *The Tonight Show, Good Morning America, The View,* and other national television shows, and has been profiled in the *New York Times, People, USA Today,* and the *Washington Post.* A native of Miami, Florida, and a graduate of Cornell University (where he founded the campus humor magazine, the *Cornell Lunatic,* still publishing to this day), he lives in Los Angeles.

HATEM ALY is an Egyptian-born artist and cartoonist who currently lives in New Brunswick, Canada, with his wife, son, and more animals than people. When he is not dealing with pets or staring at blank pieces of paper, he illustrates stories, such as the Newbery Honor book *The Inquisitor's Tale.* He is occasionally seen dipping a cookie in a cup of tea while he reads.

IT'S TIME FOR

My name is Rafe Khatchadorian, and if there's one thing I know, it's how to stay out of trouble.

JUST KIDDING!

If you're in ~~jail~~ middle school now, or will be soon, my stories could help you survive. But even if they don't, you'll probably laugh your butt off reading about all my crazy adventures!

BUCKLE UP, FRIEND. WE'RE IN FOR A RIDE!

rrroll

SPLAM!

SLAM

We're Bick and Beck Kidd,
treasure hunters extraordinaire!
It's so cool being part of a family that sails
around the world, looking for amazing artifacts
and being chased by bad guys.
You don't want to miss a single one of our
epic adventures around the world!
JOIN US! READ THE WHOLE
TREASURE HUNTERS SERIES.